A Pattern of Secrets

Lindsay Littleson

pokey
hat

First published in 2018 by Pokey Hat

Pokey Hat is an imprint of Cranachan Publishing Limited

Copyright © Lindsay Littleson 2018

www.lindsaylittleson.co.uk

ISBN: 978-1-911279-26-6
eISBN: 978-1-911279-27-3

@cranachanbooks

cranachan

Praise for

A Pattern Of Secrets

Lindsay Littleson's heart is in this story and
readers will find their own emotions engaged from
the opening pages. From the historical Rowat
family and the fictitious Muir family, she has
woven a tapestry of kinship, loss and compassion
that not only illuminates a period of the past but
has poignant resonances for today.

Robert J. Harris

You might also enjoy...

The Wreck of the Argyll
by John K. Fulton
Dundee, 1915: Nancy and Jamie uncover a deadly plot
by spies to sink HMS Argyll.

Charlie's Promise
by Annemarie Allan
A frightened refugee arrives in Scotland on the
brink of WW2 and needs Charlie's help.

Fir for Luck
by Barbara Henderson
The heart-wrenching tale of a girl's courage to save her
village from the Highland Clearances.

The Beast on the Broch
by John K. Fulton
Scotland, 799 AD. Talorca befriends a strange Pictish
beast; together, they fight off Viking raiders.

Punch
by Barbara Henderson
Runaway Phin's journey across Victorian Scotland with
an escaped prisoner and a dancing bear.

The Revenge of Tirpitz
by M. L. Sloan
The thrilling WW2 story of a boy's role in the sinking
of the warship Tirpitz.

To all the Pollok/Gibson clan,
in loving memory of Meg Pollok

Chapter 1

Jim

Ma's voice, ragged with panic, tore through my dream. I woke with a start, heart racing. Then lay, still as death, and listened.

'We've no choice.' Dad's words seemed slurred, and I guessed he'd been drinking.

'D'ye think for one moment this is what I want?'

'But we can't, Frank. You can't mean it! You're a skilled weaver. The poorhouse isn't for the likes of us!'

So, my father *had* mentioned the poorhouse... I thought I'd dreamt it; but this was real, and more terrifying than any nightmare.

Our one-roomed flat was spooky with shadows, lit by a single, spluttering candle. Ma stood by the range, twisting her apron in her hands. Her face was pale, her eyes wild in the candlelight. My father slumped in Ma's rocking chair, his head in his hands.

I tried to shout, but choked, as though someone had

1

me by the throat.

'The poorhouse?'

Ma spun round, her face contorted with anger.

'You're meant tae be asleep!'

I stumbled to my feet, stung by the injustice. My brother, Andrew, rolled over in the truckle bed, taking our shared blanket with him. He murmured in his sleep, oblivious to the fact his world was about to be turned upside down.

'I *was* sleepin', but I was woken by a' the yellin'. It's a wonder you haven't woken the whole street wi' your racket.'

Stomping over to the window, I stared out. Apart from a skinny cat, St James Street was empty, the light from the gas lamps pooling on wet cobbles. Rain pattered against the glass; wind whistled through the gaps in the frame. This flat wasn't in great shape, but it was all we had. And now it seemed, we'd lost it.

'Go back tae bed, Jim,' sighed Ma. 'You're no helpin', standin' there wi' a face like thunder.'

I turned on her, anger masking my fear.

'Stop takin' this out on me, will you? I'm no' the one to blame! If we're in a hole it isn't my fault.'

'Oh, we're in a hole, alright.' My mother jerked her head towards my father, huddled in the rocker. 'He dug it himself and now he's burying us in the same bleedin' plot.'

I grabbed my father by the shoulders, desperate to shake him back to sense.

'Dad, what's goin' on? What's happened?'

My father raised his head. His eyes brimmed with tears. My stomach clenched as I watched the tears glisten as they spilled, unchecked, down his gaunt face. I took a step back and wiped my hand on my shirt, as though Dad had a disease I might catch.

'We're behind wi' the rent. Six months behind.' Dad's voice sounded dull, leeched of hope. 'And I cannae get a job, can I? Nobody needs a weaver these days.'

'Maybe you should've stayed out the pub,' said my mother sourly. 'And we wouldn't be in this mess.'

Dad's face twisted. He half rose, his left hand raised, as though he was about to strike her. I stepped in front of my mother, more than ready to fight him, but she put a hand on my shoulder.

'I can fight my own battles, lad,' she said. 'Sit down, Frank, an' stop your nonsense.'

My father did as he was told, and slumped back down in the rocker, muttering.

'D'ye think a couple o' pints would have made any difference? We were sunk the moment that auld swine Rowat shut the factory.'

My mother rolled her eyes.

'You could have tried harder. It's your bleedin' pride that's been the ruin of us!'

My baby sister whimpered, and then started to wail in her cot, small fists beating the air. Her crying brought on a fit of harsh coughing. Ma gestured at the cot.

'Look what you've done now!' she roared.

I stood over Dad, glaring at him; taking over as chief accuser while Ma went to tend the baby.

'There has to be something we can do! Have we nothing left of value to sell?'

Dad flung his arm out, swept the room.

'It's all gone; the mantel clock, the lustre jug, your grandfather's pocket watch. They were all sold months ago. There's nothing left but poverty and debt.'

There was such despair in his eyes that I shivered.

'Go back to bed, lad,' he sighed. 'We're being evicted in the morning, so you might as well rest while you can. I've made a pig's ear of everything.'

Shock turned my voice to a feeble echo.

'We're being evicted in the morning?'

'I tellt you, go back to bed! And take that insolent look off your face, while you're at it.'

For hours, I lay on the truckle bed, leaving Andrew with the blanket, waiting for dawn. Dad snored in the rocking chair, ugly grunting snores which filled me with fury. I wanted to punch my father into wakefulness, force him to listen to my baby sister's hacking cough. How would fragile little Agnes survive in the poorhouse? What could we do to stop this disaster from happening?

But the bitter truth was I could do nothing. I worked as a piecer at the Clark Mills, but twelve-year-old lads got paid pennies. My wages couldn't save my family from losing their home; couldn't save us from the poorhouse.

The sheriff officers came in the morning. They lugged wooden mallets with them, ready to break down our door, but we were already standing outside in the street. Ma couldn't bear the thought of being dragged out of the flat.

'It's best to go quietly. There's less chance of anyone getting hurt. I might be tempted tae push one o' them o'er the banister.'

We stood in a grim huddle, watching as our belongings were flung on a cart, to be taken away and sold to pay the rent arrears. That's what the men said, though the carelessness with which they were chucking our things around suggested they thought it was all worthless junk.

Andrew tugged at my sleeve.

'Why are those men taking Ma's chair? Did Ma say they could have it?'

'Yes, of course. You know Ma. She said they could give it to an old lady who needs a comfy chair to rest her bones.'

I scanned the street, knowing that the neighbours were watching, seeing curtains twitch and hearing window sashes being dragged open.

Old Mrs Martin from downstairs leaned out of her window.

'Thievin' swines! Huv ye nothin' better tae do than bully wimmin and weans?'

The pity in her eyes made my cheeks burn with shame.

How could Dad have allowed this to happen?

My mother kept her head lowered, ignoring Mrs Martin, and clucking over Agnes, who was tightly swaddled in Ma's patched plaid. The rain had stopped, and early sunlight was glancing off the wet cobbles.

'At least it's near summer,' Ma said, scavenging for some good. 'It would be terrible to be made homeless in the chill of winter.'

Andrew stared at her, eyes round.

'We've got a home. It's upstairs. Can we go back in now? The men are going away.'

He pointed at the cart, rumbling down St James Street, carrying my family's meagre possessions: Ma's rocker, the scrubbed pine table, the rag rug, the kist.

'No, son. We're not going back. We're going to a new home instead. You'll like it. There are lots o' other boys and girls there too. Come on, we'd better go. We've entertained the neighbours long enough.'

She hoisted Agnes up, tied the plaid tightly round her waist and started walking along St James Street, towards Causeyside Street. Her chin was tilted, and defiance glittered in her eyes. She looked fierce, like she'd have decked any neighbour who dared to come out to mock us.

Dad and I trailed after her, heading to the poorhouse as though we were going to our deaths. I carried our few spare clothes, bundled in an old sheet. Ma tried to answer all of Andrew's million questions, but Dad was too lost in his own misery to speak. He trudged along, cloth cap pulled low over his head, head so bent that he kept bumping into people.

As we walked past Paisley Abbey he grabbed my arm.

'Jim, I've left my things in the upper close. Go back and get them for me, there's a good lad.'

I raised my eyes to the heavens, spitting rage, and was about to snarl at him to get his things himself, but then changed my mind. A last few minutes of freedom, some time alone, seemed suddenly precious.

'I'll catch you up,' I told Ma, handing her the bundle. I started running, back towards St James Street.

Warm May sunshine was driving the chill from the morning air. Tradesmen went about their business, opening their shops, putting out their boards, as if this was just an ordinary day. But when I reached our building I found evidence that our homelessness was only too real. The front door of our flat had been boarded up and there was an eviction notice pinned to the splintered wood.

I read it, best I could, and then looked around for Dad's

precious 'things'. They weren't hard to find, abandoned by the privy door, tied in a small hessian sack. I snatched the sack up, rage making me careless; Dad's wooden shuttle fell out and clattered to the ground.

The shuttle spun like a child's toy on the stone floor and shot down the stairs, bouncing off each step. Guilt-ridden, I chased after it, and found it wedged against Mrs Martin's doormat. I picked up the shuttle and felt the wood, smooth against my fingers. With my eyes closed I could lose myself in memories: see the shuttle at work, flying across the loom in our old cottage; clicking rhythmically as it zoomed across the warp threads.

My father had been upset the day we left our previous house, a weaver's cottage, over two years ago, when I turned ten. His family had lived and worked there for decades and it was a hard decision to leave. There'd been a crack in Dad's voice when he spoke, but his eyes stayed dry, his optimism unwavering

'We're saying goodbye to freedom, lad. No more working for ourselves. But this job at Rowat's factory is a godsend. At least I'll be able to put food on the table, eh?'

He'd run his hands across the loom like a musician playing a harp. I'd been hopping from one foot to another, keen to get going, to leave life as a draw boy behind me. I'd crouched for hours underneath that bleedin' loom as a youngster, drawing down cords to raise the warp threads, helping my dad weave Paisley shawls. At the end of each day, my knees would be so stiff and my back so cramped it was a struggle to stand straight. Weaving was my father's joy, not mine.

'Sure, Dad. It'll be better, you'll see. You'll have a steady wage. No more waitin' to get paid for commissions.'

It'll be better… I couldn't have been more wrong.

I slipped the shuttle back into the sack, stuffed my memories in with it.

As I started back, I saw a four-wheeled carriage and two hansom cabs parked at the far end of the street. It looked as if another family was leaving home too, judging by the number of trunks and cases piled on the steps of the building; an elegant sandstone townhouse. But it didn't seem likely those folk, with their posh luggage and their own carriage, were being evicted.

To be honest, it wasn't the luggage or the vehicles which drew my attention. It was a horse. One of the carriage horses was a beautiful chestnut colt, unblinkered, with gentle eyes and a silk black mane. He snickered, and flicked his tail in my direction. I'd nothing to give him, but crossed the road to say good morning, thinking it might be my last chance to greet a horse for a while.

As I stroked the horse's nose, whispered nonsense in its ear, I heard a girl's voice, so loud and urgent that it carried down the street.

'Please, Papa! Why do we have to go?'

My view was blocked by the carriage and all I could

see was a buttoned leather boot, stamping so hard that last night's rain splattered skyward.

A man answered, his voice warm, but tinged with weariness.

'We must go, dear, because you are almost twelve, and Miss Arbuckle insists you need a more feminine influence.'

'Miss Arbuckle talks a lot of tripe!'

The man sighed.

'I'm afraid for once she may be right.'

'Miss Arbuckle loathes children, you know she does!'

'Nonsense, my dear. She adores children, particularly on toast, or baked in a pie. Come on now, in you get! Hold your sister tightly. Don't let her fall!'

I stepped back from the horse. It was time I got back to my own family. As I crossed the road, I turned for another look at the chestnut colt, and saw the girl's face instead, blurry through the cab window. Afraid she might see me staring, I looked away. Her problems were none of my business anyway. I had more than enough worries of my own.

By the time I caught up with my family, they were almost at Calside. My father was trailing behind. He took his small bundle, without a word of thanks, and walked on, stumbling like a blind man.

I took his arm, both to steady him and so I could

whisper in his ear. Seeing the shuttle had stirred a memory, and I had a gut feeling the memory could be important.

'Dad, what did you do with Ma's shawl? The one you made on the loom just before we left the cottage? It was quality, wasn't it? We could sell it now. It must be worth a few shillings.'

My father's head drooped, almost to his chest.

'He took it. Did I no' tell you?

What was he on about?

I tugged his sleeve, trying to rouse him.

'I'm talkin' about Ma's shawl, you eejit!'

My voice rose, and shook with fear and desperation.

'Remember? It was meant to be a present for her birthday, two years back, and you never gave it to her. Did you sell it for drink money? Where's the shawl, Dad?'

He raised his head, but his eyes were dazed and lifeless.

'He took it. I tellt ye. I'll get the money back one day, somehow.'

Irritated by his rambling, guessing I was wasting my time, I let his arm drop. I strode ahead of him, lifted Andrew up onto my shoulders and took our bundle of clothes from Ma.

'What's wrong, Ma?' asked Andrew. 'Your eyes are awfy red. Are you no' well?'

'I'm fine, son. Just a wee bit tired with a' this walkin'.

Agnes is a dead weight an' your dad's no' bein' much help, is he? At least I've got my big lads to help me.'

She patted his head, tightened her grip on baby Agnes and tried to smile, but it was more a grimace.

I looked behind, at Dad shuffling along in the gutter, the hessian sack hanging limply from his hand. In truth, my father had been gone for months, sunk in unreachable despair. We'd lost him, somewhere along the way.

It was only when we turned the corner and I saw the high walls and the iron gate of the Abbey Poorhouse that it struck me. This was real. This was happening, and there was no way out.

I turned to Ma.

'What happens now?'

When she told me, I wished I hadn't asked.

Chapter 2

Jessie

Tense as wire, I glanced behind me, but there was nobody about. Miss Arbuckle was sewing in the parlour. Esther, our housemaid, was busy in the kitchen, helping prepare dinner. Papa had taken my brother and sister for an afternoon stroll in the town's Fountain Gardens. I wasn't likely to get a better chance than this one.

I crept up the stairs, avoiding the creaky third step, then froze at the top when I heard the kitchen door slam. Esther's boots clattered across the hall. She flung the parlour door so wide, it rattled on its hinges, reminding me of Papa's comment.

"*Esther likes the world to know she's coming.*"

'Would you like your sherry now, ma'am, or when Mr Rowat returns from his walk?' shouted Esther, who seemed to assume Miss Arbuckle was stone deaf.

'I'll have it now, of course, you stupid girl!'

I screwed up my eyes, hating that she was being

13

rude to Esther. Miss Arbuckle prided herself on being 'plain spoken'. My brother Bobby asked her once if 'plain spoken' meant the same as rude, which didn't go down well.

'How can I enjoy my sherry when I am surrounded by those infernal children!'

This comment neither surprised nor offended me. Miss Arbuckle was as fond of us as we were of her. Esther loathed Miss Arbuckle too. I overheard her in the kitchen last week saying that she couldn't stand being in the same house as 'that frosty-faced mare' and that if it wasn't for 'dear Mr Rowat and those poor children' she'd pack her bags and sail home to Ireland.

Unlike Esther, I didn't have a home in Ireland to sail to, but I'd rather have lived in a broom cupboard than in Rosehill House with Miss Arbuckle. When I told Papa so, he smiled and said we wouldn't all fit in a broom cupboard, and living at Rosehill was the best solution for the time being. But it wasn't the best. It seemed the worst thing in the world.

I crept along the top landing, watched by stern faced portraits of ancient Rowats. Great-Great-Uncle Thomas looked down his nose at me, his eyes a piercing blue.

My hand shook as it touched the handle. I gave the door a gentle push. It swung open. Dust motes danced in a beam of sunlight, glinting on the waxed floorboards and brass bedstead. Despite the fact this was my father's bedroom, a floral quilted eiderdown covered the bed. I wondered if perhaps Papa didn't feel completely at home here either.

Mama never slept in this room, my head knew that, but my heart was hopeful that in here I would find something of my mother's that would stir hidden memories, bring her back to life. The image in my head was beginning to fade and it scared me. At night I lay and worried that, in time, I might forget her completely.

There was the portrait Papa had hung in the parlour, of course, portraying Mama as a nineteen-year-old newlywed. She looked so young and beautiful, elegant in blue silk, her dark hair piled high on her head. In the painting, titled Margaret Downie Hill 1864, my mother stared straight ahead, stiff as a mannequin, her eyes serious and determined.

I kept sneaking glances at that portrait, from behind a book so I didn't get spotted by Miss Arbuckle, who was as beady eyed as a hawk. I looked into my mother's face and wondered if she guessed that tragedy awaited her; if she had any inkling that she'd be dead by twenty-eight, and that she'd leave her children motherless. And I always ended up deciding that while she does have sad eyes, who wouldn't, having to stand so long in one spot to get one's portrait painted?

But the painting didn't help me remember how Mama used to snort with laughter when Papa told one of his dreadful jokes, or recall the smell of her perfume when she tiptoed into our cosy nursery to kiss us goodnight. And I was desperate to remember. I missed her so much, and I was tired of pretending I was fine, for the sake of Papa and the wee ones. The older I got, the more I missed having my mother around.

Once in the centre of the bedroom, I sniffed for traces of her scent, but the air smelled only of soot from the fireplace and of Papa's cologne. It wasn't a shock. This wasn't Mama's house, although the mahogany dressing table and the bedstead were from our old home in St James Street. Maybe Papa had kept some of her smaller, more personal belongings? I couldn't bear the thought that her precious things had been left behind or sold. Moving out of our family home last month had been awful enough. I'd felt I was being dragged away from Mama, all over again.

Terrified of being overheard by Esther or by Miss Arbuckle in the parlour below, I slid across the floorboards, tiptoed over the rug. But my heart plummeted when I saw that the dressing table was bare, except for a collar of Papa's and a candlestick. My mother's bottle of rosewater and orange flower, the pewter powder jar and the miniature pomade tin were gone. It had been stupid of me to imagine otherwise.

My mother's silver hand mirror and hairbrush sat on my own nightstand, elegant and out of place next to my flannel and toothbrush. Papa had insisted I should have them, being the elder daughter. I'd have preferred the pomade tin, but didn't like to say, particularly as Papa had been crying as he handed over the hairbrush and mirror.

Feet clattered in the downstairs hall, making me jump.

I knew it was probably Esther, taking Miss Arbuckle her sherry, but I was panicking so much that my heart thudded in my chest. I was all too aware that I shouldn't have been sneaking around in Papa's bedroom. Esther would box my ears if she caught me snooping.

Miss Arbuckle's voice bounced off the parlour walls, echoed up the stairs through the open bedroom door. I stood stock-still and listened.

'Don't stand there gawping! Bring me the tray!'

I wished Miss Arbuckle would stop telling Esther off. No wonder Esther hated her. Bobby said that one of those days Miss Arbuckle would push Esther too far, and she would get bashed over the head with her own walking stick. But I thought I understood Esther better than Bobby. She might have grumbled, but she would bear it, no matter how badly Miss Arbuckle treated her. At least, I hoped she would, because we all needed Esther. She might have been paid as a housemaid, but she was as close to a mother as we had.

'That's a stingy measure of sherry! Did you not think

to bring the bottle, for goodness' sake, girl! Or has Cook been helping herself again?'

There was a resounding crash as Esther set the tray down on the table.

'Cook may have used a small amount for the sherry trifle, ma'am.'

'Trifle? A likely story!' Miss Arbuckle snorted. 'The woman's a lush! And where's that child; the female one William left behind when he went out? Is she suitably occupied? The devil makes work for idle hands, you know!'

'Jessie's never idle. She's a good, sensible girl; unlike that daft brothers of hers. She'll be sewing or reading in her room, ma'am,' said Esther. I whispered a thank you, but my gratitude died with her next sentence. 'Perhaps you'd like Jessie to read aloud to you for a while, ma'am?'

Noooooooooooooo! How could you, Esther?

'I'll finish this thimbleful of sherry first. Close the door, girl. There's a shocking draught. I will catch pneumonia and you'll be held responsible.'

Esther returned to the kitchen, banging the door behind her. I groaned, floored by the awful prospect of reading aloud to Miss Arbuckle.

Knowing I was about to be summoned to my doom, I turned to leave the bedroom. But then my eyes fell on a sumptuous, richly patterned cloth, draped over a high-backed chair. As I stared I realised what I was looking at.

Lying over that chair was my mother's precious Paisley shawl.

An old memory flooded my brain. I closed my eyes and saw Mama sweeping into the hall of our old house, dressed to the nines; I pictured Esther wrapping the shawl round Mama's bare shoulders, telling her she would catch her death without it. The shawl's long, multicoloured fringes trailed down the back of her plum silk crinoline. Mama smiled at us, and told us to behave for Esther, and then floated out into the night on Papa's arm.

I tiptoed over and, with one finger, traced the familiar teardrop patterns. The colours were exotic: French indigo, crimson, madder, and forest green, the material gloriously soft and silky. When I breathed in, I was convinced I could smell rosewater and orange flower. I lifted a corner, and that's when I noticed the peculiar marks, stitched into the shawl's reverse side.

I lifted the cloth further, and then dropped it as though it was burning my fingers when I heard Esther shouting my name.

'Jessie! Get your carcass downstairs! Your aunt wants you to read to her!'

Miss Arbuckle was *not* my aunt; she was my father's cousin. We were scarcely related. She swooped into our lives like a witch on a broomstick when Mama died.

And she'd never have thought of the reading if you

hadn't suggested it, Esther Jardice.

Now I had to waste an hour of my life reading one of Miss Arbuckle's ghastly melodramas, occasionally dodging out of her reach to avoid getting smacked by her stick for crimes such as "*mumbling*" or "*mangling the English language*". If I could only have persuaded her to listen to *Alice in Wonderland* or *Little Dorrit* the torturous experience would have been more bearable.

Teeth gritted, I slipped out of the room and shut the door behind me. As I walked downstairs, my fingernails dug into my palms. All I needed was five minutes, but I never got a moment to myself in this house. Somehow, I needed to find another opportunity to get into that room, and read the secret message my mother had hidden in the folds of her shawl.

Chapter 8

Jim

As soon as Dad signed his name on our admission papers to the Abbey Poorhouse, the full horror of our situation emerged.

'Sae, your older boy is twelve, is he? And whit age is the younger?' The matron was tall and angular, her mousy hair pulled back so tightly that her face looked stretched. Her teeth were rotten, and her breath was vile, reeking of onions.

'He's seven.' Ma's voice sounded strangled. 'He's only seven.'

Andrew opened his mouth, keen to announce his forthcoming eighth birthday.

'Owww!!! What did you pinch me for, Jim? That was sore!'

The matron's eyebrows knitted.

'If there's any doubt about the boy's birth date, I can check the parish records. Francis Muir an' James Muir:

21

follow the porter tae the male block. You'll be put in the admissions ward until you've been health checked,' she snapped. 'Janet, Agnes, an' Andrew Muir, come wi' me.'

'Can I no' say goodbye to my husband and son?' pleaded Ma. Her eyes were red-rimmed, and grief was etched on her face. She clutched at my arm so tightly her nails dug into my skin.

'You know the rules. As long as you're resident here, you're no' permitted any contact wi' your spouse or male children o' eight and o'er. If that rule's broken, you'll be out on your ears. Get movin".

Andrew shook his head, his black curls flopping across his eyes.

'I want Jim tae come! Jim, you need tae come wi' us!'

The matron scooped him up. He wriggled in her arms, screaming.

'Your brother isn't comin', so you can stop that carry on. Weans are seen an' no' heard in here.'

I launched myself at her and tugged at my brother, trying to wrench him away.

'Leave him alone, you auld witch!'

Two burly warders appeared and grabbed me by the arms.

I had to watch in helpless horror as my family was torn apart.

Ma, Agnes and Andrew were herded away; I was left with Dad, who just stood there, head lolling forward. We were led down a long corridor into the laundry room. The warders ordered us to strip and put on a striped cotton smock and trousers like a prison uniform.

'Come on, Dad,' I urged, trying to pull the trousers up over his calves. He continued to gaze at the laundry's tiled floor.

'Do you want me to clip yir heids?,' asked the warder. 'It's up tae you, but it would be a wise move. Place is loupin' wi' nits.'

He gave his own scabby head a vicious scratch. I placed a protective hand over my own head. There was no way I was going to let them take my hair.

'No' me. I'll tie mine back. But do his,' I said, gesturing at my father.

My father stood there and watched, unblinking, as his white hair floated like snowflakes on to the tiles. He seemed determined to pretend he was somewhere, anywhere else than the Abbey Poorhouse. It was hard to blame him.

We spent a week in the probationary ward. Then we were moved to the main block. Dad's shaved head, striped uniform and stoop-shouldered despair made him almost indistinguishable from the other inmates. Our dormitory was cramped; the privy stank and the beds were filthy and bug-ridden. The inmates were a rough bunch, and I kept Dad clear of them. They'd have stolen all the food from his plate, given half a chance.

For several weeks, as May turned to June, I endured my new life quietly, though my brain ached with the effort of thinking up escape plans. I was determined not to drown in misery, like my Dad. I was determined to get out, somehow. When I felt myself beginning to sink, I pulled myself up, imagining life outside. The apple trees would be shedding their blossom in the Fountain Gardens; the rhododendrons in the park would be bursting with glorious colour.

The work was tedious: picking oakum from tarry ropes, sweeping floors, making coir mats, but at least I was kept busy, and it was no worse than mill work. The rations were meagre and the food disgusting, but we ate enough to keep us from starvation. If my mother and my siblings had been with me, I could have endured it, but without them, life seemed almost unbearable.

Then unbelievably, our situation took a turn for the worse—much, much worse.

'Come on, Dad. You need to get out of bed.'

I could hear the irritation in my voice. He was becoming even more lethargic than usual and I'd had to take over most of his chores.

'It's your turn to peel the potatoes in the cookhouse.'

My father leant over the side of his narrow cot and vomited all over my bare feet.

I did my best, I really did, to nurse him, holding a

bowl under his chin while he spewed, replacing his soiled bedding, but I couldn't fight disease in this dirty, overcrowded place. He got worse, feverish and sweating, unable to keep anything down.

My father wasn't the only one who suffered. The dormitory gradually emptied as men and boys were carried off to the sickroom. I was terrified that my mother and the wee ones were ill too, maybe dying, just out of my reach, so begged the warder for information, but he refused to tell me anything, just spat on the ground and went to walk away.

Tam O'Neill grabbed his sleeve and gestured at my father's cot.

'Muir needs tae be moved tae the sickroom, or taken tae the Infirmary,' he growled. 'He'll infect the rest o' us.'

My body tensed, prepared for a fight. My father wasn't going into the sickroom. He'd never get better in that hellhole.

The warder pulled away from Tam.

'There's nae room, or he'd have been taken there yesterday. An' he's no' bad enough for the Infirmary. He's staying here.'

'No' bad enough? What are the rest like?' gasped Tam.

I looked down at my father, grey-faced on the cot, a thin trickle of saliva dribbling from the corner of his mouth. He seemed to be deteriorating very fast.

'I'll go an' get you a drink, Dad,' I said, trying to keep

the tremor from my voice.

My father reached out, clutched my arm. There was still strength in his grip. He pulled me towards him, and I could smell decay on his breath.

'I'm dying, lad.' His voice was a ragged whisper. 'You need tae get out o' here; try an' get it back.'

'I got your things back, Dad; remember? I dropped the shuttle, but I put it back. Everything's there, safe in their storeroom. Don't worry.'

I tried to release my arm, but his grip tightened. He raised his head, neck scrawny as a chicken's, wild eyes staring into mine.

'I mean the money. The five guineas Rowat took. I didn't tell you when it happened, because what could a wee lad like you do? But everything's changed. What have we left tae lose? You need tae get out o' here, get the money back, for your mother's sake an' the wee ones.'

'Dad, what are you talking about?'

And he told me the whole story, his voice hoarse, each word a painful gasp.

'You need tae get it back, Jim. Promise me you'll get it back.'

'I will, Dad. Don't worry. I'll get the money back. I'm no' scared.'

My father's head fell back on to the mattress. He lay there, eyes staring at the ceiling, and I waited for him to tell me more... then realised the gasping breaths had stopped. My father was dead, and I was alone in the men's building. Strangely, the terrible feeling of isolation was more painful than the grief I felt at my father's death. I was almost relieved to see him lying there, calm in death. Perhaps I did all my grieving for Dad long before he died.

Later that night, I lay awake, listening to the snores of the paupers and the howls of the inmates in the adjoining lunatic asylum. If I had to live alone, I decided, I'd rather be alone anywhere else but the poorhouse. And if I was to have any chance of getting my family back in my life, then I had to leave, and try and make good on my promise.

I threw off my patched blanket, and slipped out of bed. My father's few possessions, still in their hessian sack, would be lying in the store, along with my clothes. Tomorrow, Dad's things would be taken away and burnt. And if I escaped in my poorhouse uniform I would be accused of theft and the police would be called. Somehow, I had to get into the storeroom.

I tiptoed barefoot out of the dormitory, into the long corridor which led all the way to the main entrance. I went as far as the warden's room, and then stopped, heart thudding. The warden was supposed to be on night duty, but I could see him through the glass, snoozing on a chair. Stealthy as a burglar, I slipped past, each breath catching in my throat. As I approached the main entrance, my steps slowed. The front door was bound to be locked, and the matron wore the keys, jangling on a chain around her waist. And how could I get past her, if she was still at the front desk, working on her accounts, as she often did, late into the night?

But the store was next to the main entrance, so I needed to take the risk.

The door to the storeroom was unlocked, but that was because there was somebody inside, rummaging through people's personal possessions, dropping items of interest into her deep apron pockets. I stared, open mouthed, as the matron rifled through an inmate's jacket. She spat on the ground, nose wrinkled in disgust, when she pulled out a filthy handkerchief. Then she walked to the back of the store, her boots clicking on the tiles, and climbed onto a step stool, bony arms raised to reach a high shelf. Scarcely breathing, I crept into the store behind her, scanning the shelves. They were labelled alphabetically. The matron might have been a thief, but she was an organised one. There was Muir, stacked between Moss and Mullen. Grabbing my father's sack and my neatly folded clothes from their shelf, I scrambled out, slammed the door and turned the key in the lock. There was a long, terrible silence, then a clattering of feet. The doorknob rattled. A thud, and a muttered curse, as the matron's bony shoulder thumped against the door. I feared it would fly off its hinges, but it held fast.

'Let me oot, or I'll tan your hide!'

The matron's voice, sharp with anger, sliced through the wood.

I stepped back, fear making my heart race, my mouth dry.

'Who's there? Who did this? *Tell me!*'

Her voice was hoarse now, frayed with fear.

No way, you auld witch.

The only sound was the ticking of the clock above the desk. Listening to it slowed my heart rate, steadied my breathing. I had to ignore the matron's malevolent presence. I had to get out of here.

To the left of the entrance was a small lobby, with a sign instructing people to wait if they had an appointment, and ordering them not to spit and to keep their feet off the chairs. I'd noticed the room when I was on floor sweeping duty. Tugging off my uniform, grateful to be free of the scratchy fabric, I abandoned my smock on the floor, slid up the sash window and clambered out, breathing in the familiar smells of the town. It was bliss to be free of the reek of oakum and iodine.

Shivering in the chill night air, I pulled on my own clothes and ran through Paisley's dark streets, until I had no breath left in my lungs. Then I dropped my father's bundle and sank to my knees on the cobbles, my body shuddering.

What on earth was I to do next? How could I save my family, when I had no job, no money and no home?

Chapter 4

Jim

After living rough for a week, I found I could fall asleep just about anywhere. Waking up was the worst part. On the eighth day, I was curled like a woodlouse on a damp stone floor, until a man roared, loud enough to scare the dead.

'Did I no' tell you last night that this doorway isn't a dosshouse, you manky wee so-and-so?' The baker's heavy jowls vibrated with every word. 'Get lost, before I kick you into the Cart!'

I scrambled to my knees, groggy with sleep, but awake enough to want to avoid another kicking.

'Och no, mister. Don't do that. That river's mingin'. I was only havin' a kip.'

The baker's bulk filled the doorway. Purple-faced, he aimed a clumsy kick at my bundle and then leant down, so close that I could smell stale beer on his breath.

'If I see you again I'll call the polis, I'm warnin' you.

And take your rubbish wi' you!'

'I'm goin'! Leave my stuff alone.'

I snatched up my bundle, terrified in case the baker tossed my father's belongings into the river. The Cart stank, of human waste and who knows what else.

Afraid he was going to hurt me, I made a break for it, scurrying between his legs before he had time to aim another kick. Once free, I straightened up, flung my bundle over my shoulder and raced off along Thread Street towards Abbey Bridge. When I was a safe distance from the shop I stopped and spun round to face my enemy.

'Oi Fatty! Stop eatin' a' your own pies, you crabbit auld git!'

The baker shook his fist, but he didn't try to chase me; I'd guessed he wouldn't. The man had better things to do than chase homeless lads round Paisley. He had a shop to open, a cheery smile to paint on for his customers, fresh bread and pastries to bake.

Thinking about food was a big mistake.

As I crossed the bridge, I was hardly aware of the scummy water swirling below; visions of food were filling my head: round loaves of crusty bread, juicy meat pies dripping with gravy, crumbly treacle scones, sticky gingerbread...

My stomach growled. I groaned and clutched at my guts, trying to remember when I'd last eaten. It had been midday yesterday, when I'd cadged an oatcake and wormy apple from Mrs Martin, our ex-neighbour in the downstairs flat in St James Street. I hadn't wanted to ask, but hunger had won over pride.

I'd knocked and waited for the old lady to shuffle to the door.

'Good afternoon, Mrs Martin,' I'd said. 'I hope this fine day finds you well. I was wondering if you had any food to spare?'

'Well, is it no' James Muir! What are you doing here? I thought... Och, come in, son, and I'll see what I've got in the press.'

I'd followed as she hobbled into her one-roomed flat, feeling bad that I was taking from someone who had so little.

'Have these, lad. I'm sorry I've no' got more for you.' Mrs Martin had patted my hand as she handed over the apple and the oatcake.

'How's your Ma, son?' she'd asked, as I crunched on the apple. 'Is she coping alright in there? I was tellin' Mrs Wilson the other night that the Muirs were the best neighbours I ever had. I tellt her how heartsick I was tae see that lovely family brought sae low.'

I'd hated when she said that, hated to see the compassion in her rheumy eyes.

I knew I couldn't return to Mrs Martin's, no matter what.

Dawn was breaking, and the rising sun's pale rays glimmered on Paisley's buildings, bathing the Abbey in a rosy light. This time of day was when the town looked its best. Harsh daylight showed up soot blackened stone, horse dung splattered on the streets—the noise and filth of a busy industrial town. And at night, when Paisley's cobbled wynds were lit by hissing gas lamps, the buildings loomed, dark and forbidding, and scavenging rats scurried through the back courts.

Where now?

The questions formed as I sprinted down Orchard Street, dodging a snarling dog and Mrs Lyle's bucket of slops. *What will I do today? Where will I go?*

The answer buzzed in my brain, impossible to ignore, an insistent wasp.

Rosehill.

I kept walking, westward along Causeyside Street, past the shops with their green awnings and window displays, the tenement flats and the rows of old weavers' cottages, where the click of the handlooms and the sharp whirr of the shuttles had been silenced by the coming of steam power and the factories. I kept going, until the buildings started to thin out at Calside and green fields stretched in front of me. I stopped and breathed in clean air, then stared at the house on the far side of the cobbled street.

Rosehill was a handsome, sandstone detached house,

set well back from the road, one of several villas in this part of town which I knew were owned by the Rowat family. And this was definitely where William Rowat lived. All I'd had to do to find his address was ask a cab driver, tell him I was running an errand for the Rowats.

'Which of the Rowats would that be? Mr William? He lives in St James Street. Och, wait a minute, no he disnae. He moved last month. Rosehill House in Calside.'

I peeped through the wrought iron gates. The blinds were drawn. The children were still in bed. Someone was up though, a young woman with a fierce expression and a tangle of red hair, strands of which kept escaping from her cap. She was crouched on the wide steps at the front door, scrubbing away.

I'd seen this woman earlier in the week and hadn't been able to work out her place in the family. She looked like a housemaid, from her untidy appearance and plain frock, but I'd seen her in the front parlour after dinner, dandling the wee one on her lap, playing cards with the other two children. Perhaps she was their mother, though the weans looked nothing like her.

The woman looked up, as though her attention had been caught by a noise. She straightened, rubbed her back as though it ached like fury and threw the scrubbing brush into the bucket with such force that water splashed over the steps.

Then she abandoned the bucket and hurried inside.

I took my chance, tugged the gate open and slipped behind the huge beech tree by the garden wall. It was no bother to climb, particularly since I'd figured the easiest route to the top. From my nest in the tree I could check their routines, come up with a plan for getting in that wouldn't get me caught red handed.

There was a lot of coming and going, even so early in the morning: the postman arrived with a clutch of letters, the butcher's boy walked up the drive with his basket, the milkman stopped his cart at the gate. All of them walked round to the back door with their deliveries. The front door stayed shut.

Yawning, bone-weary after a night in the baker's shop doorway, I had to force myself to stay awake, scared I'd fall from the tree and crack my skull, afraid that I'd miss something important. It started to drizzle, and I was thinking about giving up, when the front door opened and the children tumbled out. My eyes strained to see; I was nearly as hungry for information as I was for food. Were they in good moods, or would the girl be crabbit, the wee lad greeting? He didn't seem to like school and all week had seemed reluctant to go. I couldn't understand why the Rowats forced him. Surely the lad's future was already mapped out? The Rowat family were as rich as kings—anyone with eyes could see that.

'Come on, Bobby! We're going to be late!' called the girl. There was something eerily familiar about her voice.

Bobby stomped down the front steps and scraped his boots along the path, leaving deep grooves in the gravel. When he spoke, his voice was sulky.

'But I told you, I'm not well. I've been sneezing all night.'

'I hope you've brought your handkerchief then. Mr Summer will belt you if you sniff in class.'

'But I might have something catching. It could be a fatal disease like measles or the plague or *new-moan-ee-ah!*'

The girl took his arm, and propelled him down the drive.

'I think you'd have other symptoms, Bobby, like a rash, or suppurating boils. Look, why don't you take your gird with you? It's lying on the grass over there where you left it.'

Bobby ran to fetch the hoop, and they hurried towards the gate, unaware they were being watched, their conversation overheard.

The red-haired woman appeared at the door.

'Jessie, you've left your lunch! You'd forget your head if it wasn't sewn on!'

'Thank you!' Jessie raced back to the house, her long plaits flying.

I filed this information. The woman was Irish, going by her accent. The girl's name was Jessie. I already knew the boy's. He was Robert, Bobby for short. The girl seemed sharp with the wee lad. It made me glad I didn't have an older sister to boss me around. But I wished I had clothes like Bobby's; a warm moleskin jacket, soft velveteen breeches, leather boots. My own shirt was thin as paper, and my trousers were ragged.

As they reached the gate, the girl struggled with the bolt. I had to make myself stay where I was, not jump down, not try and give her a hand, as a friend would. I had to keep reminding myself. These children were not my friends; Jessie and Bobby Rowat were nothing to me. My mission was to break into their house and take back what their father stole from mine.

Chapter 5

Jessie

The school bell clanged, and Bobby pushed past me, desperate to get out.

'Freedom!' he yelled. 'And the holidays are nearly here!'

I clattered down the steps of Paisley Grammar behind my brother, grateful that the school day was finally over. It was a lovely summer's day and the classroom was hot and stuffy, the windows too high up to enable me to see outside. It was lovely to breathe fresh air and feel the sunlight on my face.

'I'm faster than a steam engine! Watch me go!'

Bobby spun his gird and hurtled after it down School Wynd, his metal hoop clattering on the cobbles. I decided to pretend I didn't know him and walked sedately down the cobbled street, doing my best to be ladylike.

My ladylike behaviour didn't last five seconds. Bobby, too engrossed in bowling the gird, veered off the narrow pavement onto the road, right in front of the coalman's cart. My hands flew to my mouth and my books thudded onto the pavement. I screamed, a high pitched, blood-chilling sound.

Time seemed to slow down. Somehow, I had time to wonder how on earth I would explain to Papa that Bobby had been fatally injured while I was minding him, when there was a shout from behind the cart.

'Watch the wean!'

The driver glanced to the side, saw what was happening. He tugged sharply on the reins and the cart pitched to the left. Its massive metal wheels rolled past my brother's head, missing him by inches.

'What do you think you're doin', you eejit!'

But Bobby was oblivious to the driver's yells. He swerved back onto the pavement and continued following his gird down the hill.

My whole body trembled with shock. I'd thought he was a goner. He was a wee devil to give me such a fright. But I could see he was fine: completely unhurt. Esther always said Bobby had more lives than a cat.

I was in no hurry to reach the bottom of School Wynd, so I took a few moments to reassemble my books into a tidy pile and then I sauntered down the hill, gazing in shop windows, thinking that I should have given some of my books to Bobby to carry. That might have kept him out of mischief.

Bobby waited, bouncing with impatience, at the bottom of the cobbled street. His shirt was untucked, the detachable collar loose. His fingers were ink stained and his freckled face smeared with mud. He looked more like a street urchin than the beloved only son of a respectable Paisley merchant. As I approached, he waved a stubby finger in the direction of Gilmour Street Station.

'I saw him, Jessie! I saw the burglar again! But he saw me looking and ran for it. He went that way!'

I scowled at my brother, who leapt up and down like a jack-in-the-box, oblivious to my annoyance.

'Hush, Bobby. Calm yourself. You're scaring the horses with all that bouncing around. Stop your nonsense.'

'It isn't nonsense.' Bobby stopped jumping and his lip jutted. 'I told you, Jess. I saw a burglar sneaking around in our garden yesterday and now he's following us.'

I raised my eyes to the heavens. Bobby was becoming obsessed with burglars. Yesterday, when Papa took our little sister Mary to visit old Mrs Coats, Bobby ran in the house shrieking that there was a stranger in the garden. Esther and I ran outside straight away. Old Tam was hoeing the vegetable patch and swore he hadn't seen a soul. He said the only person in the garden was Bobby, and he'd just told him off for trampling on the begonias. But Bobby insisted he'd seen a stranger, so we checked the garden from one end to the other. There was definitely nobody there. But all last night my brother wouldn't stop going on about burglars and now he was doing it again.

Bobby shook his head, tears spurting like geysers.

'Old Tam's blind as a bat; he wouldn't have seen a burglar if he walked over his feet!'

When I didn't answer, his frustration grew. His face reddened and he stamped his foot.

'And of course, he wasn't there when you looked. Burglars don't wait around to get caught, do they?'

'So how did this man get out of the garden, Bobby?' I tried to resist the urge to take Bobby by the shoulders and shake sense into him. 'The back gate was still padlocked.'

'He must've jumped over the wall. And I didn't say it was a man burglar. It was a boy. He had curly hair and brown skin. His clothes were dirty. He had bare feet and he was carrying a sack for all his loot.'

It was a detailed description; very believable. But Bobby's stories tended to be detailed. He loved the elaborate lie and I had fallen for too many of them recently.

'Bobby, it's too high a wall to jump over. Why don't you stop being silly and just admit this is another of your stories?'

'I'm not lying! I'm telling the honest truth! Why do you never believe me?'

'You said you were telling the honest truth when you claimed your school cap had been eaten by bears,' I reminded him. 'And then it turned out that you'd stuffed it under the hall chest. There were no bears involved. Not a single one. And you weren't being entirely truthful with Mr Summer when you told him last week that you were late for school because you'd been kidnapped by pirates. You'd sneaked off to the corner shop to buy sweeties.'

Bobby kicked a pebble into the gutter.

'I saw a man with a patch on his eye. He might have been a pirate,' he muttered.

'Miss Arbuckle says you're the *Boy who Cried Wolf*. You have told so many fibs, nobody believes a word you say.'

My brother wiped at his eyes with his jacket sleeve.

'I don't tell lies. I have a creative brain. Papa says so.'

'That's because Papa has a kind heart and always thinks the best of people. The rest of us think you're a lying wee toad.'

Bobby glared at me and I felt bad for calling him names. He was only seven after all.

'You're the meanest sister in the world! *I hate you!*'

He threw the gird down so hard that it clanged on the cobbles. Then he ran off. I watched him go, and made no attempt to call him back. Bobby stormed off on a regular basis and I had given up worrying about his whereabouts. He'd be heading back to Rosehill, there was no doubt about that. He never missed his dinner.

I picked up Bobby's gird and cleek and was tempted

to fling them into the river to be on the safe side, just in case he succeeded in getting himself run over by a tram next time, but decided against it. He was furious enough with me already.

There was some traffic on Causeyside Street; the rag and bone man's cart, a couple of horse drawn trams, a few carriages. A beggar huddled in a shop doorway, his cap at his feet.

'Spare a penny, miss?'

His raised fingers were black with dirt and there was spittle in his beard. I hurried past him, trying not to grimace at the smell of him.

All the way to Calside, I kept stopping and looking behind me. I had a peculiar, unsettling feeling of being followed, but every time I looked, there was nobody there.

Chapter 6

Jim

County Place was mobbed with hansom cabs, and I used them as cover, jinking and dodging round the stationary vehicles. As I reached the station, I slowed down, because I had no option. I felt as though I was dying. My heart was thumping in my chest, my side was aching and sweat soaked my armpits. The soles of my feet were calloused, hard as leather, but even so I had managed to cut myself on a sharp stone. Blood oozed between my bare toes, mingling with the grime. The pain made me feel sick and dizzy.

I couldn't believe I'd let this happen. I'd been seen again. I might have ruined everything. The boy was bound to tell his sister and then all hell would break loose.

First thing that lassie will do, I thought bitterly, *is shout for the polis. They'll haul me back to the poorhouse before I've time to blink.*

45

Panicking, I dived behind a pillar and leant against it, gasping for breath. My lungs felt as though they were about to burst, and I hadn't run far.

A uniformed man strode across to the station entrance. He was heading straight for me.

Is it all over? I wondered. *Am I goin' tae be arrested?*

But then I recognised the railway uniform.

'Move along!' shouted the guard, waving his arms at me, as though he was trying to swat a troublesome midge. 'This area is for passengers and staff only!'

'How do you know I've no' got a ticket? I could be gettin' a train to Timbuktu for a' you know.'

The guard scowled. He had a sharp, weasel face.

'I'll give you *Timbuk-bloomin'-tu!* Get along with you!'

'I'm goin'. Don't you worry about me. I'll get the bleedin' tram to Timbuktu. It'll be quicker than your stupid trains.'

Toe gouping, I limped off. Pain burned my lungs, and my mouth was sandpaper dry. I couldn't see along New Street to the bottom of School Wynd, so had no idea if the Rowat children were still there. I didn't want to crash right into them, so I pretended I was leaving, but, as soon as the guard's back was turned, I sneaked behind another pillar and slid to the ground, waiting for my breathing to return to normal and the ache under my ribs to ease.

A year or two ago, I used to be able to race my pals all the way from the St James Street flats to the Clark Mills and back, no problem, but recently my strength seemed to be seeping away. I peered at my skinny wrists, pawed at my thin neck. *Maybe I was actually dying.* I'd hardly eaten for a week. But when push came to shove, I'd rather have starved to death than gone back in the poorhouse. Worn out, I leant back against the pillar and closed my eyes. I couldn't go back there, couldn't give up, no matter how bad things got on the street. I needed to get my family out.

The problem was, all I'd managed to do in my week of freedom was survive, and even that hadn't been easy. My piecer's job had been filled, so I was having to scrape by on casual work. I hadn't saved a penny. And I hadn't kept my promise to my dying father. My future, and my family's, rested on me getting into Rosehill without being caught and getting out again with the money.

My brain spun in dizzy circles. The man's voice seemed to come from a long way off.

'You look done in, lad. Are you ill? Can I get you some water?'

My eyes flicked open, on the alert for a kicking. Polished leather shoes, a silver tipped cane. I looked up. A tall, bearded gentleman was standing in front of me, smartly dressed in a double-breasted frock coat and topper. His pale blue eyes were kind. I tried to speak, but my mouth seemed as knotted as my brain.

'I'm not, sir. Not ill, I mean.'

'Are you hungry, perhaps?'

'Aye, but I'm no' the only one. Times are hard, sir.'

The man nodded, as if he understood. But, clocking his silk cravat and gold watch chain, my jaw clenched. What could someone like him know of hard times?

'Harder for some poor souls than others, I am sorry to say,' he said. His voice was sombre and resonant, like a minister preaching a sermon. 'It's an unequal society and we must all work hard to improve it.'

'That's easier for some than others. Work's hard to come by, particularly for weavers and their kin.'

The man flushed: his eyes shifted from my face. He cleared his throat and when he spoke, his voice cracked.

'Yes, times are particularly hard for those poor souls. I'd like to assist you, but I'm afraid that I have no small coins on my person.'

'I'm not begging! I was minding my own business. It was you who came up and bothered me! I'm only having a rest an' then I'll be on my way.'

'You'll cope better with travel if you have food in your belly.' The man rummaged in his attaché case, still not looking me in the eye. 'Here, take the remains of my luncheon. I've had more than I need.'

He pulled out a bottle and a greaseproof packet, handed the items to me and strode out of the station, before I had time to say thank you.

I checked the curly writing on the label, in case the stranger was trying to poison me, and then gulped down the bottle's contents. The elderflower cordial smelled faintly floral and tasted deliciously sweet and refreshing. Then I stared at the greaseproof paper package. Was this a con trick? Was the man getting on his train now, sniggering about the stone he wrapped in paper and handed to a homeless urchin?

Steeling myself for disappointment, I ripped open the packet. In it, untouched, nestled a soft wheat roll, slathered in butter and piled with chunks of cheese. Wiping away tears with my sleeve, I bit into the bread, ravenous as a stray dog.

When I'd licked the paper, mopped up every crumb of bread and cheese, I was surprised how much better I felt, how much more energy I had, and how my focus returned.

I stood up and keeked round the pillar, checking that the coast was clear. Of course, the girl and the wee boy would be long gone, but I didn't need to follow them too closely; I knew exactly where they lived. I'd been there several times and could have found Rosehill House with my eyes closed. Yesterday evening, I'd walked right round the outside walls of Prospecthill House to reach the back of Rosehill. I even scaled the wall and got into the back garden. And what a garden! I'd never seen anything like it; velvety, blood-red climbing roses, honeysuckle arches, trellises and meandering paths. There was even a fish pond. But it was a bad mistake to go in daylight. The old gardener didn't notice me at all, but I was spotted almost right away by the boy. Luckily for me, the lad ran inside the house, screaming about burglars, and I took my chance and scarpered, shimmying up the wall like a sweep up a lit chimney. It was pure luck that I wasn't caught. Next time I went over that wall I'd have to go in darkness. Next time, one way or another, I would be entering the house.

I should have been more careful today, but to be fair, what else could I have done? The wee fellow was running under the wheels of a cart. It would have been heartless to stand and watch it happen. What else could I have done but dart from my hiding place, yell at the driver to swerve? But when Bobby's eyes met mine, I knew I'd been rumbled. He recognised me right away. Robert Rowat was no fool, whatever his sister might think.

It was stupid to hang around outside their school; pointless to follow the Rowat children home. But I felt tugged, like thread on a shuttle. Sometimes my blood boiled with fury that those children seemed to have everything I lacked; a large comfortable home, parents, an education, enough to eat. But then the girl would laugh at her brother's antics and I'd find myself smiling too, and wishing I knew her better, sure we could be friends: which was daft, of course. We could never be friends. We might have lived in the same town, but we had nothing else in common. Our only link was that her father stole from mine.

Swinging my bundle on to my shoulder, I set off. I'd go and have another look at Rosehill. Just once more. And on Sunday night I'd get inside the house and get the money back—or die trying.

I had to, because in four days' time, my little brother was going to turn eight. And on his birthday, he'd be torn away from my mother and moved to the men's block.

Chapter 7

Jessie

When Esther banged the dinner gong I jumped with fright.

'Oh, no,' I whispered to my reflection. 'I hoped he'd be back by now. I thought he'd be too hungry to stay away.'

My hand trembled as I tried to do up the tiny buttons on the back of my dress. In the mirror I could see tears brimming in my eyes. I'd have to tell Papa. I couldn't sit at the dinner table and pretend everything was fine.

For one thing, I'd need to think of a believable reason for Bobby's absence, and he was the one with skills in the fibbing department. I'd already checked all the places he might have hidden himself: the garden shed, the pantry, the laurel bushes. He wasn't in any of them. He hadn't come back to Rosehill.

My insides churned. As the eldest child, this disaster felt like my responsibility. And if I was being totally honest, I *had* been unkind to him. It *was* my fault that he ran off.

There was nothing else for it, I had to go down and tell Papa that Bobby had run away, and I was unable to find him. But I needed to fasten myself into this hideous grey taffeta dress first. Miss Arbuckle wouldn't be one bit concerned about Bobby, but she'd have a fit if I failed to change for dinner.

As I walked downstairs to the dining room I wondered if Mary Queen of Scots felt such an awful sense of impending doom on her way to the executioner's block.

Grandma was sitting at the head of her mahogany dining table. She was dressed, as always, in an old-fashioned bombazine crinoline, her grey hair scraped back in a bun and covered by a widow's cap. Grandma Rowat's style was very much modelled on the Queen's. A smile wreathed her wrinkled cheeks when I entered.

'Here you are at last!' she said. 'How lovely that you could make it! Was it a wearisome journey? Did you come by hansom cab or carriage?'

Grandma always seemed delighted to see me, but she had a tendency to forget that we were both related and resident in the same house.

Papa patted her hand gently.

'It's Jessie, Mother: your granddaughter. She lives here now, remember?'

Esther was arranging cushions so that little Mary could reach the table, but Mary wasn't happy with her seat. She shrieked and waved her pudgy fists.

'Beside Papa!'

But Papa was sitting to the right of Miss Arbuckle, and Bobby—a wicked grin on his freckled face—was sitting on his left.

My eyes bored into my brother's. I wanted to screech like a banshee, fly at him, shake him until his teeth rattled.

I tried to send a silent message.

Where have you been hiding, you mean little toad? You scared me half to death!

If I spoke aloud, then Papa would want to hear the full story and I preferred not to tell him about the near accident in School Wynd. He had plenty of worries without that. Anyway, Miss Arbuckle would not have appreciated me screeching at the dinner table. I'd have been sent upstairs to the nursery and I was far too hungry to go without dinner.

'Bobby tells me he has been playing hide and seek since you got home from school,' said Papa with a smile. 'He says that you haven't been able to find him.'

'In my day, children were given chores,' grumbled Miss Arbuckle. 'No time was ever wasted on play. Play is a ridiculous new-fangled notion. No good will come of it. Mark my words.'

I was too focussed on Bobby to take the bait. I glared at my brother.

'I've been searching high and low, Papa. It was as if he'd vanished into thin air, but no such luck, I'm afraid. He has come back, like a bad penny.'

Papa's smile faded.

'This seems to have been a strangely ill-tempered game of hide and seek. Tell Jessie where you were hiding, Bobby. Don't leave her in suspense.'

Bobby's eyes darted between Papa and me. He could see the furious look on my face and he wasn't grinning any more. When he spoke, his tone was mutinous.

'I climbed into the beech tree in the front garden, way up in the top branches. You could have found me if you'd looked up!' As I slid into my seat next to him he whispered. '*It's where the burglar hides.*'

'Oh, shut up about the stupid burglar!' I hissed, kicking him under the table, so hard that tears sprang into his eyes.

'It is, though. He hides in the beech tree. I saw him!'

I kicked out again, but I misjudged the distance. My boot connected with Miss Arbuckle's thick twill skirt and she shrieked.

'Ouch! William, one of your ghastly offspring kicked my leg!'

She gave Papa a frosty look, as if everything was his fault.

'There really was no justification for begetting so many children, William,' she said, her voice as icy as her eyes. 'A single child—preferably a quiet, female one—would have been quite sufficient. But having had such a brood, the very least you can do is keep them under control!'

Papa sighed.

'Bobby, be a good lad and keep your feet still when you're at the table.'

'That boy will come to no good!' snapped Miss Arbuckle. 'Mark my words! *Spare the rod and spoil the child!*'

Bobby wiped at his face with his sleeve. He didn't reply, even though he must have been furious about being blamed unfairly. Shame burned my cheeks, but I was too hungry to admit that it was me who'd kicked Miss Arbuckle.

My father looked round the table, clearly mystified by our miserable faces.

'Cheer up, my dears! Cook is about to produce another splendid repast. Aren't we the lucky ones!'

Bobby, for whom the prospect of food always pushed every other thought from his head, pulled a face.

'Clucky, more like. It's been chicken for dinner since we came here.'

'Ah, yes, but chicken in so many different guises,' said Papa, his eyes twinkling. 'Isn't that so, Jessie? How many different recipes for chicken dishes have we counted this month? The woman's a marvel!'

I smiled at Papa, despite myself.

'Cook's a veritable genius with poultry. This week alone we've had roast chicken, boiled chicken and a tasty chicken pie.'

As I talked, I felt my shoulders relax. There was no need to upset my father. Bobby was safe. All was well.

'Yes, but I'm sick of chicken! Doesn't Cook know how to make anything else?' wailed Bobby, just as the door opened.

Cook, short, fat and crabbit, stomped into the dining room and plonked a large tureen in the centre of the table. Then she turned and glared at Bobby.

'Chicken Fricassee,' she announced, and lumbered out, her nose in the air. I thought I heard her mutter "*ungrateful little wretch*" under her breath, but I might have been imagining it.

Esther carried in bowls of boiled potatoes and diced carrots and served up our meal. Mary wriggled so much with excitement that she fell off her cushion. Esther rushed to prop her back up again, giving her a quick cuddle as she did so.

'Sit still, Mary, dear,' she said. 'If you're a good girl, I'll give you the wishbone from the chicken.'

Miss Arbuckle frowned and pointed at Esther's front.

'There's a stain on your apron, girl. And these potatoes aren't properly cooked,' she snapped, stabbing at them with her fork. 'They're rock hard.'

Esther rolled her eyes behind Miss Arbuckle's back.

'I'll let Cook know, ma'am. Mary, don't spit out those carrots. They're good for you.'

'Hoddible,' muttered Mary, spitting orange gloop across the table. She was the only one of us who wasn't afraid of Miss Arbuckle.

'What an impertinent child! I despair of your children's manners, William, I really do.'

Papa lowered his fork, a mischievous grin on his face.

'She's only imitating her elders. Poor Mary isn't to know you're the only one in this household with permission to insult the vegetables.'

I had to disguise my snort of laughter with a cough.

After dinner we retired to the parlour, for '*family time*'. Mary played with her dolls and Bobby noisily re-enacted the Battle of Balaclava with his tin soldiers. Miss Arbuckle tutted at his antics, and attacked a sock with her darning needle. Grandma Rowat sat in her favourite chair by the fire, hemming a handkerchief, while I perched beside her on a footstool, practising embroidery stitches on a sampler. I'd begged to be allowed to embroider poppies on a sash to brighten up my grey dress, but Miss Arbuckle had refused saying, "*Poppies, indeed! I think that one forgets the maxim that children should be seen and not heard.*"

Mack, Grandma's grumpy West Highland Terrier,

was curled at our feet. A tremendous crash made us all jump, like startled hares. Papa dropped his newspaper and leapt to his feet.

'Are you alright, my love?'

Little Mary was sitting on the floor by the window seat, looking sweet and innocent in her white organdie frock. She was surrounded by shards of broken china.

'It's bloken,' Mary lisped, stating the obvious. 'Big clash.'

Miss Arbuckle put a hand across her eyes.

'She's going to pretend to faint again,' I murmured.

Papa rushed over and scooped Mary up, checking her body for cuts.

'The little one's perfectly fine, thank goodness!'

He set her down and patted her bouncy ringlets.

'That may well be, William, but your mother's precious vase is smashed,' snapped Miss Arbuckle. 'What is wrong with the child? Why can't it sit still? Perhaps you need to feed it less frequently. Hush, Mack! Stop that infernal racket!'

She waved the sock she'd been darning in our direction.

'Off you go upstairs, the lot of you. Leave your poor father in peace.'

I took Mary from Papa's arms, but Mary, realising she was being taken up to bed, resisted, wriggling like an eel and kicking out.

'Nooooo! Blankie!'

'I'll get your blanket if you stop kicking me.'

I walked over to the window seat and picked up Mary's tattered comfort blanket. As I turned to leave, Mary heavy in my arms, I glanced out of the front window. The sun was low in the sky and the beech tree cast a giant black shadow across the lawn. I looked up and felt my heart stop. I squinted, unsure of what I was seeing. Was that a face, peering through the leaves? Was somebody up there, sitting in the crook of the branches? Was it possible that my brother had been right all along?

I shivered, feeling chilled to the bone despite the warmth in the room. If Bobby was right and we were being followed home and spied on, then something deeply sinister was going on. I stepped closer to the glass, straining to see.

When my father put his hand on my shoulder, I gasped, startled.

'Are you alright, sweetheart? You've gone quite pale.'

'I thought I saw something up there, in the tree.' I pointed at the uppermost branches.

Papa stood beside us, one arm round my shoulders, and squinted up at the beech tree.

'I think I see what you mean. It'll be the tawny owl, Jess. He roosts in that big beech. Did you see his big round eyes gleaming? He gave me quite a fright when I came home late the other night; stared down at me

60

and then hooted so loud that it seemed as though it was right in my ear. Here, give Mary to me and I'll carry her upstairs. She's too heavy a lump for you.'

He lifted Mary out of my arms and swung her onto his shoulders. Bobby grabbed him around the waist, I hung from one arm and Papa lumbered round the room while we shrieked with laughter. Miss Arbuckle shook her head, tutted her disapproval and stabbed her needle into the sock.

'It was never like that in my day. Children knew how to behave.'

I took one last look out of the dining room window, trying to take comfort from Papa's words. I couldn't see anyone or anything up in the tree branches. But I couldn't shake off the feeling that something very weird was going on at Rosehill.

Chapter 8

Jim

When I nodded off, my foot slipped and crashed through the branches, sending twigs and leaves floating to the ground. I jerked awake and grabbed on to a bough to stop myself tumbling to earth.

Hiding up here in a tree's getting naught done, I thought, angry with myself. *It has to stop. I should be in town, looking for night work.*

Cramped and weary, I stretched, trying to get rid of the pins and needles in my arms and legs. But I didn't move from the tree. There was something safe and comforting about hiding up there, where no one could reach me, gazing into the windows of Rosehill, watching a well-off family get on with their comfy lives and enjoy their free time. All that week though, I was aware I was being an eejit. I'd been imagining that I was part of their world, living in Rosehill, playing soldiers with wee Bobby, winning at cards, and chatting to Jessie, who I guessed was about my age.

But when I leant forward and peered through the foliage, I saw Jessie looking out of a ground floor window. She was staring up at the tree, straight at me. A chill breeze blew through the branches and I shivered, filled with an uncomfortable awareness that I was behaving badly. I *shouldn't be watching this family. This isn't my life. These people are none of my business. All I need to do to keep my promise to Dad is get inside Rosehill House and straight back out again with his money.*

But I was still watching when the gentleman in the window swung the little girl onto his shoulders and my mouth twisted with the effort of holding back tears. I could remember so well going to the Fountain Gardens with Dad and getting a "*cokey back*" all the way home to the cottage. I'd bounce along on my father's shoulders, gripping on for dear life—feeling on top of the world.

Grief and loneliness gnawed at my guts, as painful as hunger.

I missed Dad, but it was a comfort to know he was at peace, out of his misery. I missed the rest of my family more. I needed to go and visit them, no matter how scary the prospect. As soon as that decision was made, my heart felt lighter; the ache in my stomach eased. I turned and looked in the opposite direction. Down the hill, below Paisley's Water Works, I could see the roof of Abbey Poorhouse.

I'm coming to see you, I whispered. *I'll no' be long.*

Stuffing my bundle into a hollow in the beech's trunk, I slid down from the tree, slipped out of the gate and started walking back down Smith Street, towards Calside. My teeth were gritted; I felt determined as a terrier, but with no clear idea of how I was going to succeed.

A church clock chimed the hour. Seven o'clock. The poorhouse inhabitants would be outside in the airing yard, getting some fresh air before lights out. This was as good a moment as any.

Working out my plan as I walked, I turned down a lane and entered the poorhouse by a different route than I'd left, by climbing over the wall; surely, I thought, the first person in history to willingly enter that hellhole.

Slinking along the wall, keeping an eye out for the matron and the porter, I slipped into the laundry room. It was empty, which was just as well, as I hadn't worked out a Plan B. Even Plan A was a roughly sketched outline. Plan A's success rested on me looking as little like a boy as possible. How I was going to achieve that was anyone's guess, but if I was going to get to see my mother it was essential, because as long as Ma was an inmate, she and I weren't permitted to see each other, as I was male and over seven years old. The rules of the Abbey Poorhouse were legalised cruelty, which made them a pleasure to break. The question was, how?

I scanned the laundry shelves. I'd been hoping for a

plaid, or a large shawl, to wrap myself in, but there was nothing like that here. There were neat piles of laundry: bed covers, smocks, shifts, aprons, baggy trousers. I tugged a shapeless grey shift from one of the piles and quickly pulled it over my head. The fabric was like sacking, so rough it scratched my cheek. I looked at my reflection in the copper wash tub and shook my head. Plan A wasn't working. I looked like a twelve-year-old boy in a horrible dress.

I searched the shelves again, helped myself to a grey cotton headscarf, and tied it under my chin. I looked at my reflection again and was more pleased with it. I made a bonny enough girl now, with my black curls peeping out under the headscarf and my long dark lashes. All I needed now was courage, and some luck.

Heart thumping, I strolled into the female airing yard and leant against the wall, in what I hoped was a girlish pose, and looked around.

The majority of the female inmates were old; poor souls, worn out by overwork and poverty. They hunched on benches, waiting for death, wrinkles etched into their leathery skin. But there were young women in there too; girls kicked out of domestic service for falling pregnant, or abandoned by their husbands and left destitute.

In the centre of the yard, two lassies were squabbling, pulling at each other's hair, ignored by the older women.

As I looked across the yard, I could feel panic rising

and my breath caught in my throat. Where was my mother? Where were my little brother and sister?

They had to be there, because if they weren't in the airing yard, they were in the sick room or the plague pit. That thought was so unbearable, that my stomach cramped, and I felt lightheaded.

Then I heard an off-key tune I recognised.

'*Clap yer handies till daddy comes hame!*'

I moved a few inches, and I saw her. My mother was crouched in a corner of the yard. I hadn't been able to see her at first because those screeching lassies had been in my way. I let out a long, slow breath and whispered a thank you, though I had no clue who I was thanking.

My mother was singing, sort of; teaching wee Agnes a clapping game.

As I watched, a smile tugged at my lips, remembering her singing the same song to me. Ma's a terrible singer. It was Dad who could hold a tune, once.

Ma pulled Agnes on to her knee and clapped hands with her, while Andrew recited the rhyme. Ma's black curls were flying loose from her headscarf as she clapped and bounced Agnes.

'*Clap yer handies till daddy comes hame.*
Daddy has siller but mammy has nane,
Clap yer handies till daddy comes hame!'

Then her voice cracked and faded. I guessed she'd realised her song choice wasn't the best.

Dad wasn't coming home any time soon.

My feet were glued to the ground. I hadn't known what to expect when I came. I'd been afraid to come back, in case I found the rest of my family gone, carried off by the same disease that had killed Dad.

But here they were, safe and well.

I moved towards them, hugging the wall round the airing yard, trying not to draw the attention of the other inmates, in case I was a less convincing lassie than I imagined.

I kept my voice low.

'How's it goin', Ma?'

My mother spun round, and her hands flew to her mouth.

She didn't answer, but threw her arms around my neck, and squeezed the breath from me. Her own breath was warm against my cheek. She smelled of carbolic soap.

'It's so good to see you, Ma. Are you an' the weans alright? You haven't been ill?'

'We're fine, but I've been worried half to death. They told me Frank was deid. And then they said you'd left...'

She held me by the shoulders and stared as though she could hardly believe I was real.

'I was afraid they were lyin' to me, and that you were deid an' all. It's been o'er a week, without a word.'

She pulled a mock angry face.

'I should clipe you roun' the lug.'

'I'd have written you a letter, Ma, but paper an' ink are hard to come by on the streets.'

A noise behind her made my mother jump. She looked round, fear in her dark eyes.

'You'll be in awfy trouble if they catch you in the women's yard. You'd better get out o' here. Are you comin' back in, Jim? I know it's terrible in here, but we're fed and clothed. You look as though you haven't eaten since you left. There's no' a pick on you. I couldn't bear it if anything happened.'

'I'm no' comin' back, Ma.'

She gripped my arm, as if she could keep me by force.

'But what are you doin' wi' yourself? Where are you sleeping at night?'

'I'm doin' some casual work in town. It's for the best. It's the only way to get you a' out of here. We're goin' to need a bit of cash behind us to start afresh.'

My brother tugged at Ma's shift.

'Ma, why's oor Jim dressed as a lassie?'

I grinned at him, tapping the side of my nose.

'This is a disguise, so the matron doesn't catch me.'

Andrew didn't look convinced. It was over a month since I'd last seen him and already he looked older, thinner, no longer a little boy, but a lad approaching his eighth birthday. Both he and Agnes had lost their soft black curls. Their hair had been shorn and their scalps were as prickly as baby hedgehogs and purple with iodine.

'Look at the state of the weans.'

Ma shrugged, acting as if it was nothing.

'The matron shaved them, to get rid of the lice. But they're content enough, aren't you, Andrew?'

Andrew stuck his thumb in his mouth, suddenly babyish again.

'Speak to your big brother, Andrew!' insisted Ma. There was a loud popping sound as she tugged his thumb from his mouth.

Andrew scratched a sore on his cheek, cocked his head to one side and considered his words carefully.

'My head had nits. Nits are very itchy.'

'You're right, they are,' I agreed, grinning at him. 'It's good that you're rid of them now.'

'Aye, but our bed has bugs. Bugs are itchy too. Look!'

Andrew pulled up his smock and showed me an ugly red rash on his stomach. I crouched down, and put my hands on his shoulders.

'Our new place won't have bugs. It'll be clean as a new pin and warm as toast, I promise.'

Ma gave me a warning glance.

'Don't put such daft ideas in his head, for goodness' sake! As I said, they're content here, despite the bugs. Andrew's goin' to learn to read, if the school ever starts. You mustn't worry about us. Look after yoursel.'

'But what about when he turns eight, Ma?'

I whispered the words, not wanting Andrew to hear me. My mother turned away, but not before I saw terror in her eyes. She was trying to keep strong for the wee ones' sakes, but she knew fine that in a few days Andrew would be dragged away to live with the men and older boys.

'I'll fix this,' I insisted. 'I've got a plan.'

She turned back towards me, chin raised.

'The best thing you can do for me is to take care of yourself. You'd better go, Jim, before Matron comes out an' gives you laldy. It was so good to see you, son. Please take care, dear.'

I hugged her, fumes of iodine and carbolic catching the back of my throat and making it sting.

'I'll come back an' get you out. We'll be together again soon, in our own place; a bug free place.'

Ma smiled, but her eyes didn't meet mine and I knew she didn't believe me. I opened my mouth to tell her about the treasure at Rosehill but then snapped it shut as the matron marched into the yard, ringing a hand bell to signal the end of the inmates' free hour. Her eyes fell on the two lassies, who were still tearing at each other's hair.

'Stop havin' a rammy or you'll be oot on your ear!' She yanked them apart. 'Line up! Hurry up noo! It'll be lights oot in twenty minutes.'

'It's mid-summer, you daft mare,' muttered one of the

old woman as she hobbled into line. 'It'll be light until eleven o'clock, whether you like it or no'. You're no' God.'

I started to edge backwards, towards the laundry, but the matron's eyes fell on me.

'Where do you think you're goin'? Get intae line, girl!'

She stormed right up to me, beetle browed, and grabbed at the sleeve of my stolen shift.

'Whit's your inmate number? Are you new? Who completed your admissions form? Speak, lassie!'

There was no point struggling. The woman was as strong as a bull. Trying not to panic, I bobbed my head and attempted a semblance of a curtsey, which wasn't easy when I was being lifted off my feet.

'My name's Rose Hill, ma'am. Yes, I'm new in this afternoon, ma'am. Mr Kennedy helped me fill in the form, ma'am.'

'Well, he should have tellt me; totally irregular. I'll be having words wi' him. Join the line.'

She let go of my arm and pushed me forward. I took my chance. I ran, dodging past the listless old women, the skinny orphans, the sharp-faced girls.

As I passed my mother, Andrew called out.

'Bye, bye, Jim!'

A grin split my face, imagining the puzzled look on Matron's face.

Crashing into the laundry room, I knocked into the copper tub and upended it. Scummy water flowed across the floor. Skidding on the wet tiles, I raced out of the back door and flung myself at the wall. I scaled it and threw myself over the top. I landed feet first on the pavement, hitting the ground with a bone-jarring shock.

I headed off, wondering where I was going to kip tonight. My heart felt lighter, having seen my family was safe, and I was relieved to be free of that place. The next time I went there, I promised myself, it would be through the front door, to take my family home. I needed to keep positive; be like my father used to be. When times got hard for the weavers Dad always encouraged us to dream of better times. Ma used to pull faces behind his back, and mutter that "*some of us have to live in the real world*". It was only when he lost the job at Rowat's that my father lost hope, let everything slip away from him. It wasn't going to be easy, putting our lives back together without Dad. But I had to try. I had to finish what he started, and get back what he lost. I had to save my little brother.

Chapter 9

Jessie

Every time I closed my eyes, I saw a face peering through the leaves of the beech tree, two dark eyes staring into mine.

Mary was sprawled like a starfish in her cot. Bobby was twitching in his sleep, muttering nonsense under his breath. His bad dreams often kept me awake, but I only had my own nightmares to blame tonight. Irritated, too hot in the stifling room, I pushed the heavy eiderdown aside and slipped out of my bed.

The room was warm as the fire was still burning, safe behind the fender guard.

I pulled the chamber pot out from under the bed and was glad to find it unused. Bobby tended to miss and sometimes the handle was sticky with urine. While I relieved myself, I became aware of loud noises downstairs. Papa and Miss Arbuckle were arguing again.

I tiptoed over to the nursery door, planning to close it

and shut out the noise. But as I reached it, another plan formed. Perhaps I could sneak into Papa's room again and have a closer look at the shawl. From the fury in Miss Arbuckle's voice I guessed their argument would continue for a while.

First, I went back into the nursery and pulled the drapes aside. When I peered through the window bars I could see that it was getting dark outside. Silver moonlight glinted on the fish pond in the back garden. A shaft of moonlight glimmered on the bronze statuette by the wall, and the fat cherub's grin looked more evil than heavenly. I listened for padding feet; for creaks on the floorboards above me, but no sound came from upstairs. Esther would hopefully be fast asleep in the attic room she shared with Cook, who, according to Esther, snored like a congested pig.

I decided that I was going to go for it. Nerves taut, barefoot, my nightgown flapping round my ankles, I padded along the landing.

Miss Arbuckle's voice ricocheted up the stairs.

'You're being ridiculous, William. Such financial imprudence!'

I had no idea what she was talking about and I didn't wait around to hear my father's reply.

Silently, I slipped into Papa's bedroom. A coal fire burned in the grate here too, but otherwise the room was in darkness. I crept over to the dressing table and used a safety match to light the candle.

The shawl was still there, lying over the chair. I reached out my hand to stroke the material and circled my finger round the elaborate curved teardrops and stylised flowerheads.

Then I tugged the shawl off the chair and draped it over my head. It was heavier than I'd imagined, and silken soft. Wearing it made me feel like the Indian princess in a book of fairy tales, gliding around in a palace in Kashmir. I pranced around the room, swathed in the shawl, pretending I had tinkling bells tied to my ankles and wrists.

But then I caught a glimpse of myself in the tall mirror. Even in candlelight I bore no resemblance whatsoever to a princess, Indian or otherwise.

Realising that I was wasting time, I dragged the shawl back over the back of the chair, annoyed with myself for being so childish and anxious to leave the shawl exactly as I'd found it, so that nobody suspected.

Then I did what I should have done straight away. I pulled up the edge of the shawl, and tried to decipher the marks in the light of one flickering candle. They could have been letters, stitched rather than woven into the reverse of the cloth, but the marks were tiny and in the same coloured threads, so they were almost impossible to read. I thought I could make out a curly, elegant 'M' and following that a loopy 'A'.

Could it be Mama? Or Margaret? Or was I imagining that these marks were letters at all?

The third stair creaked. I froze, heart thudding as I listened to the sound of footsteps in the hall. My eyes swivelled, but there was nowhere to run.

Papa strode into the bedroom, and his eyebrows shot up when he saw me standing by the chair.

'Heavens above, child, you made me start,' he said, 'Why on earth are you not in bed? It's very late.'

'I was asleep, but the shouting woke me,' I said, figuring attack might be a useful form of defence.

Papa smiled ruefully and tugged off his cravat.

'Oh dear, I am sorry. We weren't shouting exactly; nothing so undignified. It was merely a heated disagreement.'

He walked over and lifted a corner of the shawl, trailing his fingers through the long fringe.

'Were you admiring this? It's a beautiful object, made lovelier when your mother wore it. You shall have it when you're old enough to take proper care of it, my dear.'

My heart rate slowed. He wasn't angry with me after all. I was no longer sure why I'd thought he would be.

'Was it made in your factory, Papa?' I asked, knowing perfectly well that it was, but I was reluctant to leave.

'It was, but it's a very special one. It was woven by our weavers from the hair of the Kashmiri goat. I will tell you about it one day, but for the moment, if you don't mind, my dear, I'd like to have some privacy to write some letters.'

I opened my mouth, wanting to keep talking about the shawl, desperate to ask him about the marks sewn into the cloth, but Papa started rummaging in his writing stand. His shoulders were stooped, and I was suddenly frightened by the lines on his forehead, the white hairs in his beard.

I ran over, wrapped my arms around his waist and hugged him.

'Goodnight, Papa. Don't stay up too late. I love you.'

He dropped a kiss on my forehead.

'Off to bed, dearest.'

There was such sadness in his voice, but I knew I was being dismissed, so I left without another word.

The nursery was just as I left it, everyone fast asleep, watched over by Mary's creepy collection of dolls and by Wellington, our old rocking horse. I patted him on his wooden nose and climbed back into bed.

Then a small voice from the back of the dimly lit room made me jump.

'After Mary broke the jug, you saw him in the tree, didn't you? You saw the burglar, didn't you, Jessie?'

'Bobby, you gave me a fright! I thought you were sleeping. Yes, you spooked me so much with your talk of burglars that I thought I saw something in the branches, but Papa says it's only the tawny owl.'

There was silence and for a moment I thought my brother had fallen asleep. But then he whispered, so quietly I could hardly make out what he was saying.

'Owls don't wear clothes. Owls don't have curly hair. It was the burglar you saw, and I bet he's still there.'

'Hush, Bobby. Don't be so silly. Go back to sleep.'

But while Bobby was soon snoring softly, I was still awake when the birds started singing their dawn chorus in the garden. It was hard to sleep when I was afraid that a stranger was watching and waiting, out there, in the dark.

Chapter 10

Jim

Spying on the Rowat family wasn't going to keep me alive. I needed ready cash, so the next morning I headed for the George Hotel in Smithhills.

'Can I be o' service, ma'am?'

Mrs King handed me a broom and I set to work sweeping horse dung from the street outside the hotel. It was hard, smelly work and my shirt was damp with sweat by the time Mrs King pronounced herself satisfied the job had been done properly.

She handed me a copper coin, and I thanked her, though tuppence was poor pay for such hard graft. A heavy cart rumbled past the hotel's front door and Mrs King shook her head in disgust.

'No sooner does the dung get cleaned up, than another beast comes along and does its business on the road. Why can't folk ride about on them high wheelers instead? Those things might be lethal, but at least they

79

don't mess all over the cobbles!'

'But high wheelers don't have ticklish ears. They don't act pleased to see you, or nuzzle your pockets for carrots. I'd rather have a horse any day.'

She clicked her teeth.

'Aye, well, these things cost, so it's not likely a choice *you'll* ever have to make, is it now?'

Heat rose up my neck, but I didn't lose my rag. My job at the hotel was too important to lose.

'Don't you believe it, Mrs King. My ship will come in, sooner or later.'

'Is that so?'

She took back her broom and went inside, shouting for her son to come and give her a hand with the barrels.

I tucked the tuppeny bit in my trouser pocket, and spent the rest of the morning outside the hotel, collecting pennies for holding horses' reins while the carters popped inside for a drink.

But Mrs King's comment had rattled me. Her words rang in my skull.

Aye, well, these things cost, so it's not likely a choice you'll ever have to make, is it now?

Her scathing tone had made it clear that she didn't think anything would ever change in my life, and I could see why she thought like that. I was prepared to work hard, but the money wasn't ever going to be enough to do more than keep me alive. It wouldn't save my family from the poorhouse. It wouldn't save my brother from being wrenched from his mother's arms in three days' time.

I had to find those five guineas. I had to get into Rosehill House.

The afternoon was spent hanging around the soup kitchen in the Abbey cloister. Mrs Martin had told me about it when I visited her, and I went along to check if it was true—that food was being given away for free.

The place was mobbed. The smell of barley broth wafted over the crowd and I took long deep breaths, drinking it in. There were half a dozen ladies, in fancy dresses and straw boaters, linen aprons tied around their waists, standing at a long table, doling out the soup and cutting loaves into hunks. They smiled all the time, pretending to be happy, but I noticed that they wiped their hands on their aprons every time their fingers touched a poor person's.

'It's very good to see you here on this lovely afternoon,' trilled the black frocked minister, smiling at me as I reached the end of the queue which snaked round the cloister. The minister's mouth was overcrowded with teeth. 'I don't think we've met before?'

'I just came for the soup,' I told him, taking a bowl from one of the women, who ladled soup from the tureen, careful that her hands didn't brush mine. 'Thank you, ma'am,' I said, and then turned back to the minister. 'I've never been a churchgoer, an' don't plan to start now. No offence meant.'

The minister nodded.

'None taken.'

His teeth might have been as crooked as gravestones in a neglected churchyard, but this minister was far younger and cheerier than any churchman I'd ever met.

He pointed at three skinny lads sharing a bench. They were shovelling barley broth into their mouths as if they'd never tasted food before.

'You are very welcome to come here every Sunday, just for the soup. However, I would take your time,' he continued. 'Or you'll make yourself sick, as those poor fellows surely will.'

It was practical advice and I heeded it. The last thing I needed was to lose the benefit of good home cooked food. I took my time, nibbling the bread and savouring each mouthful of soup. The crowd round the soup kitchen was growing though, and I guarded my bread jealously, worried in case it was snatched out of my hand.

I was wondering if they'd mind me going up for seconds when the minister came over and sat down opposite, his eyes owl-like behind his wire spectacles. Slurping my broth, I eyed him warily.

'I was wondering, lad, if you were aware of the new Industrial School in Albion Street?'

I nodded.

'It's got a huge sign out front. It's hard to miss.'

'Yes, indeed. I thought perhaps the school might be the very place for you, eh? You'd get bed, board—and an education. How's that for a splendid notion?'

I should have guessed that would be the catch. They were trying to trap me; lock me in another institution.

'No, I've had a' the education I need, thanks. Four years at the Infant School in Lawn Street was ample. I can read anythin' I need an' my writin' is fair to middlin'.'

The minister kept smiling. He wasn't giving up that easily.

'But you need somewhere to live, by the look of you. Your clothes are in tatters and you're thin as a rake. Think of the pleasure of a warm bed at night and hot meals every day.'

'I'm workin' on that. I should be sorted by the end of the week.'

Placing my spoon back on the table, I grinned at the minister, and the minister smiled back, but his eyes were doubtful. There was nothing I could do about that. I could hardly tell him that I was planning to break into Rosehill House that very night and if I found five guineas there, I was taking them. The minister would have called the polis and they'd have dragged me off to Miss Kibble's Reformatory, no question.

Having nowhere else to go, I sat on a stone bench in

the cloister for a while, listening to the choir singing in the Abbey, wishing that I believed in God. It would have been a huge comfort to think Dad was looking down from Heaven, wishing me well, urging me on. But such things seemed unlikely. For a start, Dad wasn't in one of the carefully tended Abbey graves. His body had been wrapped in his sheet and carried off, and had probably been tossed in a pit, alongside the corpses of all the other diseased paupers. How could I believe in a God who'd allowed that to happen?

As I listened, I let go of my gloomy thoughts and let the soaring music fill my brain. The music swooped like a flock of birds, diving down towards earth and then flying skyward. I followed it, closing my eyes and listening to its echoes.

Until I felt a tingling sensation in the back of my neck and sensed that somebody was watching.

Chapter 11

Jessie

On Sunday morning, Grandma and Miss Arbuckle rode to the Abbey in Uncle Thomas's carriage. The rest of us preferred to walk rather than get our teeth rattled out on the cobbles. The service was long and deadly dull, taken by the minister Reverend Lees, with his shiny bald head and sticking out teeth.

At the end of the service, I tried to steer my family out of the doors as quickly as possible, but Grandma Rowat couldn't do anything quickly and Miss Arbuckle insisted on stopping to talk to everybody, mainly to criticise the minister's diction and lack of hair.

Reverend Lees was standing on the front steps and I was getting increasingly mortified, sure he must be able to hear Miss Arbuckle telling Mrs Jane Arthur how much she missed the old minister, when Mrs Arthur tactfully changed the subject.

'Mr Rowat, I was wondering if I could borrow your

charming daughter this afternoon.'

Mrs Arthur smiled at Papa, using her own considerable charms, for which Papa always fell. She was very elegant, lovely in a dark blue beaded dress with matching hat. 'It will only be for a little while and she will be well chaperoned. We're running a soup kitchen in the Abbey to raise funds for the new Industrial School. I wouldn't ask her to serve of course, but perhaps she could help back stage, as it were, with the washing up?'

Papa tipped his hat. He was almost as taken with Mrs Arthur as I was.

'Certainly, Mrs Arthur. I'm sure Jessie will be more than willing to further the joint causes of education and women's suffrage.'

'Excellent. I'll ensure my man drives her safely home in the trap at the end of the event.'

I smiled, oddly delighted at the thought of an afternoon's dishwashing. Sunday afternoons at Grandma Rowat's were mind numbingly dull, with bible readings and prayers led by Miss Arbuckle.

But after an hour washing dirty bowls, hands deep in a sink of scuzzy water, the prospect of reading aloud to Miss Arbuckle from the bible didn't seem as unappealing as it had. The other helper, a tall girl with smallpox scars, had landed the better job, stirring an enormous vat of Scotch broth. Bored to death, I threw down my dish cloth.

'I'm going to sneak a look outside before the next lot of dishes arrive.'

The girl stopped stirring and frowned at me.

'Mrs Arthur said we've to stay here. She said that the soup kitchen's customers are rough types.'

'I walk to school and back every day, with my brother,' I said airily. 'We see "rough types" all the time and we've never come to any harm.'

But when I peeked out the marquee's flap, I could see what Mrs Arthur meant. I'd never seen so many poor, ragged people gathered in one place before in my whole life. The only spare patch of ground next to the Abbey was crowded with men, women and children, many barefoot and dressed in patched, filthy rags. Some boys were chasing each other around in the burial yard. One man was perched on a gravestone, smoking a pipe and swigging from a bottle.

Colourful bunting fluttered across the front of the marquee. Mrs Arthur stood beside the long trestle tables, holding someone's squalling baby and rallying her troops of volunteer ladies. If she notices me, I thought, she'll be cross with me for disobeying her.

But I needed a break from washing dishes, if only for five minutes. So I squeezed underneath the marquee and headed towards the Abbey, keeping close to the wall, to avoid the crowd. The cloister was empty, and I stood behind one of the stone archways, watching. Two toddlers were quarrelling over a hunk of bread, and there was a desperation in their gaunt little faces which was terrifying. One won the bread and the other ran off crying. A group of women clad in rough aprons and plaid shawls, gathered in a huddle, their arms folded across their chests, scowls on their faces.

'Thinks she's Lady Muck, that yin,' grumbled one, jerking her head towards Mrs Arthur.

'Aye, they wouldn't have to hand out soup tae the starvin' if they paid decent wages. Wonder how she'd manage on four shillings a week. That daft hat must have cost four guineas.'

The women's ingratitude shocked me. How could they not see the kindness in Mrs Arthur's face? Didn't they know she supported Women's Suffrage? If I'd been braver I'd have gone over, leapt to Mrs Arthur's defence, but the anger and scorn on their pinched faces suggested they wouldn't listen.

The choir was singing in the Abbey behind me. I turned around, and saw a boy sitting alone under a cloister arch, a portrait in a curved frame. His eyes were fixed on the wall opposite and he was moving his hands in time to the music. His greyish shirt was torn, his hair was a mass of tight back curls and his skin was a smooth taupe. He made me think of David, the shepherd boy in the Bible, who grew up to be King of Israel.

I watched him for a moment and then tugged myself

away to go back to my sink of dirty dishes. My heel clicked on the stone slabs, and the boy turned his head. He stared, eyes round with shock.

'What're you doing here?' he asked, his voice hard, accusing.

'I didn't mean to disturb you. I'm sorry,' I gabbled, my face burning. The boy jumped up, and fear made my stomach clench. With his scowling face, he'd lost all resemblance to a gentle shepherd in a biblical painting. He looked what he was: a ragged, angry thug.

I rushed back to the safety of the marquee, anxious to return to a world where I understood the rules; a world where I belonged.

Chapter 12

Jim

When I saw Jessie Rowat standing there, staring at me, I thought it was all over. Perhaps she'd remembered me being in School Wynd, or recognised me as the spy in the beech tree. But her face flushed crimson, as though she was the one in the wrong. Just in case, I ran for it, in the opposite direction, as soon as she rushed off. But nobody called me to come back as I left the Abbey, and hurried up Smithhills. Nobody chased me as I crossed the rickety Sneddon Bridge.

I spent the rest of the afternoon earning a few pennies by helping out in the Victoria Saw Mills in Love Street, sorting and stacking off-cuts, until my arms ached and my hair was spiked with sawdust. The sawmill closed on a Sunday, but the elderly security guard let me in, and later he kindly shared his dinner of bannocks smeared with rhubarb jam. It was hard to remember the last time I ate so much in one day.

'I'll let them know you were in at the usual time,' promised the old fellow, wiping crumbs from his beard. 'But you'd better come and collect your thruppence in the morning or they might forget to pay you. You know how forgetful folk get when there's money involved.'

When I reached the Fountain Gardens, I clambered into the fountain beside the four iron walruses and gave myself a quick wash to rid myself of the dust. Then I found my favourite bench, curled up on it and dozed, planning to get up and head to Rosehill when the clock struck midnight. But, stomach full, I fell into a deep, dreamless sleep. When I woke, chilled to the bone, it was the early hours.

Furious with myself, I scrambled up from the bench.

The distance seemed further in the dark, but I was so anxious to get there before dawn that I ran most of the way, slowing down every few minutes to get air back into my lungs.

I arrived at the town's edge, where a patchwork of moonlit fields and woodland stretched in the distance. When I reached the house, I dodged past the front gate, and followed the wall, all the way round the grounds of neighbouring Prospecthill House to the back of Rosehill. The wall seemed an impossibly high barricade, but I'd climbed it before in daylight and knew how to tackle it. Heart pounding against my ribs, I started to scramble up the wall, my bare feet finding footholds in the sandstone.

Once at the top, I sat for a moment, gathering threads of courage.

The garden was lush, dreamlike in the moonlight. The fish pond glowed, silver lit. In the branches of the beech tree in the front garden, a tawny owl hooted.

My heart banged so loudly in my chest I was sure it must be audible inside the house. Thoughts zig-zagged in my brain, so fast I could hardly keep up.

The house would be locked up, tight as a drum. This was a pointless waste of time. I'd never get in there without being caught. And if they caught me, then it would be the poorhouse or the County Jail and I didn't think I could stand either.

As I sat there on the wall, afraid to move, a picture formed in my head, clear as a millpond. I was being dragged off to the County Jail in handcuffs. A baying crowd had gathered, and Ma was there too, the little ones clutching at her apron.

"Leave him be. Don't take my boy!" she screamed.

In the beech tree, the owl hooted again. I jumped, so startled that I almost fell off the wall.

The image dissolved, but Ma's words echoed in my brain.

Don't take my boy!

I thought of Andrew and shivered. I had to pull myself together. However scared I was, this had to be done.

I looked over at the house. No lights glowed in any of the windows. The shutters were drawn, blank as closed eyelids. But one small top floor window was uncovered, and sat very slightly ajar.

Taking a huge breath, as if I was about to dive underwater, I leapt from the wall. My bare feet sank in damp soil, crushing the flowers. I stepped onto the grass, fear clenching at my guts, waiting for that yappy wee dog to bark and reveal my presence.

But there was silence. The house slept on; only that small sash window keeked at me, daring me to enter.

I crept nearer, the grass spongy and cold beneath my feet.

A wrought iron drainpipe snaked down the stonework from the gutters. It passed close to the window, but perhaps not close enough. If I fell, I'd fall hard, onto gravel. But there was no other way. Ivy clung to the walls at ground level, but the old gardener kept it well trimmed. It was via the drainpipe, or nothing.

I started to shimmy up the pipe, my feet struggling to grip the slippery metal. About half way up, I lost my grip and slid six inches downward, grazing my knees on the sandstone wall, but I kept going, inch by painful inch, until finally I was level with the top floor window.

A cloud drifted across the moon and the back garden was plunged into darkness. I reached out a hand, tried to grab the window ledge. It was too far. I'd never make it.

And even if I did, I'd be dangling by my finger tips from the ledge. All I wanted was to give up, to climb down and scurry away. But then the cloud moved. The garden was once more bathed in moonlight and I could see what I was doing. I looked upwards, towards to the roof. Only a few inches higher, and then I could risk jumping down, angling my body towards the ledge. My fingers, however, seemed to have melded to the drainpipe, and my feet had frozen stiff. My spirit was still willing, but my body had stopped work, rebelled like a Sma' Shot weaver.

Panicking, I tried to force movement into my feet. My left foot jerked, and I scrabbled for a hold, dislodging flakes of paint and rust. Desperately, I clung on, my fingertips whitening as they tightened their grip. But my hands were slippery with sweat and, try as I might, I lacked the strength to hold on. Hands scrabbling, I toppled backwards and fell, plummeting in silence through the night sky. When I hit the ground with a dull thud, the breath was knocked out of me. I lay, groaning, sharp gravel biting into my skin.

The thud woke the dog. The Westie started barking, high-pitched and frantic.

Upstairs the Irish woman swore.

'That bleedin' dog! Does it never shut up?'

The sash window crashed shut, locking me out.

I lay there for a few minutes, too winded to move, waiting for the back door to open, and for the game to be up. But nobody came to see what was causing the dog to bark itself into a frenzy and eventually the animal stopped. When silence fell, it dawned on me that it wasn't all over. Escape was still possible.

Struggling to my feet, I stood for a moment, my whole body trembling with shock. Despite the throbbing pain in my back, there didn't appear to be any bones broken. I stumbled towards the wall, and decided against attempting another climb. Biting my lip to stop myself from groaning, I limped across the back garden and, hugging the wall, hobbled towards the front. As I unbolted the main gate, the eejit dog started barking again, but no lights went on in the house.

A large area of woodland was nearby and I crawled into a laurel bush. The ground felt damp against my knees, but I was too exhausted to care. At least nobody would find me here, and move me on.

Shattered, I lay down and stared up at the stars, glittering through their canopy of leaves.

I'll try again. It's not over. I'll save you.

My whispered words floated in the night sky, insubstantial as soap bubbles.

I was the eejit, not the bleedin' dog. I'd failed my family. My little brother's world was about to be shattered.

Time was running out.

Chapter 13

Jessie

Bobby pointed the footprints out to me when we got home from school on Monday afternoon.

'Look, Jess. The burglar's been here again! He must have come last night!'

I looked. Two clear prints; as if someone had jumped down from the wall into the garden.

'Bobby, did you do this? Did you take off your shoes and jump in the mud? If you get muck on the rugs Miss Arbuckle will be fuming!'

His eyes filled with tears.

'You never believe me, Jessie. Never. You're always calling me a liar. It's not fair!'

He ran inside, wailing that he hated me, that I was a horrible sister. I chewed on my lip, feeling mean and guilty. Then I stared at the prints for a few moments, and compared the size of them to my own. Now that I was taking the time to look, I could see they were bigger than

Bobby's, but not as large as an adult's. Was it possible that Bobby had been right all along, and that my eyes hadn't been playing tricks on me when I thought I saw someone hiding in the tree? Could a stranger be spying on us, I thought, and following us home? Mack had been barking during the night; he didn't often do that. What if he had been trying to scare off an intruder? Maybe I should have believed my brother, I thought guiltily. Maybe I *was* the worst sister in the world.

Later, I walked up Carriagehill with my father, wondering if I should tell him about the footprints in the soil, but not wanting to spoil his cheerful mood.

'Here we are!' said Papa, stopping suddenly, his loud voice making me start. He held out his arms, embracing the view. 'What do you think? Isn't it wonderful?'

I frowned, puzzled by his enthusiasm.

'It's going to be a fabulous asset to the town when it opens to the public.'

I looked round at the huge trees and green fields of Brodie Park, hoping I was giving the answer Papa wanted. 'Bobby will love it. But why have you brought me to see it now?'

Papa took my hand. His eyes shone. I hadn't seen him look so happy since Mama died. When he spoke his voice was gleeful, shaking with excitement.

'I've bought over four acres of this land, beside the

new park. I'm going to build us a house here, Jessie! One day we'll have a proper family home again, with a huge garden for you all to run amok in; a tree house for Bobby and Mary, a swing seat for you! What do you think of that plan?'

My eyes stung with tears, and I turned away from my father, afraid he'd think I didn't like the idea.

'That's wonderful, Papa,' I said, after a moment, squeezing his hand. 'If only Mama was alive! She would have loved-'

'I'm doing this for your mother, Jess. The house will be named St Margaret's, in her memory. It will take a long time to build, because I want it to be perfect.'

He gazed at the woodland, a small smile on his face. But I needed him to focus on the present, because I was afraid that by the time the house was finished, it might be too late.

I took a deep, gulping breath and let the words spill out.

'Papa, I always feel better when we talk about Mama. I don't think it's good for us to pretend we're not missing her. Perhaps if we talked about her more often, we wouldn't all feel so alone with our sadness.'

He smiled again, but he seemed miles away, still gazing across the woods and fields, imagining a magnificent villa, a monument to his wife.

'Perhaps you're right, my dear.'

He might not have been listening, but I figured I *was* right. I vowed that from that moment on I was going to talk about my mother whenever I felt like it. I wanted to keep her memory alive, not just for me, but for Bobby and for poor little Mary, who had no memories of Mama at all.

We stood there for a moment longer, holding hands and remembering. Then we started to walk home.

'Have you any ideas about what you would like to do with your life?' asked Papa, as we reached the front gate.

It was my turn to fizz with enthusiasm.

'I'd love to study art, father. Mr Summer says I've got a real flair for the visual arts. It's why I need to visit Italy, as soon as I'm old enough, so that I can find out as much as I can about famous artists and paintings. I don't want to be the Art School dunce, do I?'

My father laughed.

'Indeed, you do not. So, the new house will need to have an art studio too, eh?'

As we walked up the drive and approached Rosehill, my feet started to drag. I didn't feel ready to face Bobby's reproach. I didn't want to listen to Esther being bossy, or Miss Arbuckle's nasty remarks. I needed some time on my own.

'I think I'll just keep walking a little longer if that's alright. It's such a lovely evening.'

'Certainly, my dear. Off you go. Enjoy the peace, but

don't stray too far. Keep within the Rowat enclave! '

I agreed that I would, but my fingers were crossed behind my back...

It was a beautiful evening. The sun slanted through the trees, glowed on the cobblestones. I left Rosehill and kept walking, past the villas where my uncles, aunts and cousins lived, down Calside and along Causeyside Street. As I walked, I had the strange sensation that somebody was behind me. I kept turning to face an empty pavement. I'd planned to stroll through the Fountain Gardens but decided it might be safer to stay out of the park, knowing fine that I'd gone much further than my father intended.

As I reached the entrance I spun round, and I saw him.

A dark-skinned boy, skinny as a rake, with lots of curly black hair, ragged clothes. Bobby's burglar. He wasn't a figment of my brother's over active imagination: he was a real person. And I had seen him before. His was the face in the tree. He was the boy in the Abbey.

The boy tried to dodge behind a lamppost, but he moved much too slowly.

My hand shot out, gripped his wrist.

'Why are you following me?'

His arm was shockingly thin, and I let go, afraid to snap his bones. The boy took his opportunity and ran for it, so I had no option but to chase him. Miss Arbuckle would have been swooning for Scotland if she could have seen me, chasing a ragamuffin boy down the paved paths and across the manicured flower beds of the Fountain Gardens. Regular morning drill with Miss McMaster was standing me in good stead. I seemed much fitter than the boy. He was limping too, and I was gaining on him rapidly; but what, I wondered, was to be done when I reached him?

It was hardly the done thing for a respectable young lady to rugby tackle another person to the ground. Even in the privacy of the back garden, rough and tumble play was frowned on by both Miss Arbuckle and Esther. No, that wasn't quite true. It was considered perfectly acceptable, even admirable, for Bobby to climb trees and wrestle with his friends, but out of the question for the girls in the family.

It isn't fair, I muttered, as I leapt over a tidy display of geraniums and raced headlong down another path. A middle-aged couple were sitting on a bench, enjoying the June sunshine, and the lady clicked her tongue, her face taut with disapproval, as I thundered past, almost at the boy's heels.

I knew that if they recognised me, and reported me, I'd be in deep trouble. I pictured being hauled into the front parlour by Miss Arbuckle; imagined how she'd tear me to shreds.

You are a disgrace to the Rowat family name, an

unmanageable hoyden! You realise that you have rendered your marriage prospects non-existent. Your poor Mama will be spinning in her grave!

The chase couldn't be allowed to continue. There was only one thing to do. I hurtled ahead of the boy; kicked out with a buttoned kid boot. He tumbled over and landed clumsily, sprawled on the path in front of the fountain. I perched, prim and upright, on the fountain's lumpy edge, looking the perfect lady. I smoothed out my skirts and pressed one foot down hard on the boy's back, pinning him to the ground.

He screamed as though he was in agony. Alarmed that I was really hurting him, I took the pressure off, but only a little.

'Who are you and why are you following us?' I demanded. 'Was it you whom my brother saw in the garden?'

The boy struggled to get up. He squirmed under me, as wriggly as an eel. He was quite hard to manage with one foot.

'I'll let you go if you promise faithfully not to run away. You must promise on your honour.'

'I promise. I won't move. I swear on my father's life. Get off my bleedin' back!'

I raised my foot. The boy rolled from under me, scrambled to his feet and ran, jinking past the fountain, down the main path and through the wrought iron gates.

'Liar!' I screamed, at the very moment two elderly ladies strolled into the Gardens. They stared at me, and then whispered, heads together under their frilly parasols.

One of them let go of her companion's arm and glided over.

'Shouting, my dear, is most unladylike,' she scolded. 'Were you calling for your mother?'

I shook my head.

'Well, your nanny or governess, perhaps? Surely you aren't in the Gardens unchaperoned?'

I got to my feet, brushed grass from my skirt.

'I can go wherever I like, thank you very much!' I yelled. 'I'm a twelve-year-old girl, not an infant!'

And I marched off through the gates, my mouth twitching as I imagined the expression on the faces of the two old ladies.

Chapter 14

Jim

As I reached the gates, my feet dragged, shackled by guilt. I couldn't run off, with Jessie Rowat thinking I was a liar. Despite everything, I didn't want her to think ill of me. I sat on the wall by the big wrought iron gate and waited for her to come out, wondering what mood she'd be in: dejected that she let me get away, or furious?

But then I saw her; stalking out of the park, shoulders back, a triumphant smile on her face; as if she'd won—or couldn't care less that she'd lost.

When she saw me, the smile slipped. For a moment she looked uncertain, anxious. But then her eyes narrowed. She walked right up to me, and stood on the road, hands on hips. Feeling at a disadvantage, I stood too. It didn't help, because she was a good two inches taller than me. Her cheeks were flushed, her bonnet askew, her long hair tangled.

She poked her finger so hard in my chest that I staggered.

'Oi! There's no call for violence!'

'You swore! And then you ran off! You're a lying toad!'

'I'm no' a liar,' I insisted, stepping back onto the pavement to give me a bit of height. 'I swore on my father's life, an' he's deid, so it didn't count.'

The girl raised her eyebrows, gave me the same scathing look I'd seen her give her brother.

'You can try and weasel your way out, but you clearly said the words "*I promise*". A gentleman's word is his bond, my father says.'

'Does he now?' I was unable to keep the anger out of my voice. A look of alarm crossed her face, and she moved away from me.

'I'm going back to Rosehill!' she said, voice so loud I was afraid the polis might come running. 'I want you to stop following me right this minute or I shall go straight to the police, I swear it—and Rowats keep their promises.'

I could tell she meant it. I was digging a deep hole for myself. It had been stupid to wait for her at the gate. She could point me out in a police line-up, no bother. But I'd felt the need to justify myself. Like her, I always prided myself on my honesty, until my life started tumbling out of control. Now I hardly knew who I was anymore. When I lost my family, I lost part of myself.

The girl started walking away from me. Without taking time to think, I called out to her.

'I don't mean you or your kin any harm. I only want to get back what's mine!'

She whirled round and stormed back. It was my turn to step away, to avoid her clenched fists.

'What are you talking about? My family has nothing of yours, I can assure you!'

'That's where you're wrong. Your father took a fortune from mine; five guineas to be exact.'

She stared at me as if I'd said something ridiculous, as if she didn't know whether to burst out laughing or slap me into sense.

'That's utterly outlandish. It's a clear case of mistaken identity. My father's a respectable business man, not a thief.'

I shook my head.

'It isn't a mistake. I know exactly who you are. You're William Rowat's daughter. Your father's a tea importer and retired shawl manufacturer. And a thief.'

Her eyes widened in shock and it was a moment before she spoke. When she did, her voice trembled.

'You might think you know all about us, but clearly you don't know my father! He would never do such a thing! He's the kindest man in the world. He's always giving money to charity. Miss Arbuckle says he shouldn't because he doesn't know if it's going to those who deserve it, but Papa says—'

My own anger boiled over.

'I tellt you. He took my father's money! Your brother's right, you know. You never bleedin' listen!'

She stood, open mouthed. I felt my cheeks burn, knowing I'd said too much.

'How do you know what Bobby says? Have you been spying on us?'

I cringed as she stared at me, horror in her eyes.

'Streets are public places. It's a free country.'

Even to my own ears, my excuses sounded feeble.

'Yes, but you've been spying on our house, haven't you? I knew I'd seen somebody in the tree the other night! Don't you ever come near our house again, do you hear me? I'm going to tell my father! I'm reporting you to the police. You'll go to jail, where you belong!'

Despair gripped me. Why hadn't I scarpered when I had the chance? I'd ruined everything. It was over.

I opened my mouth to shout back, and a strange noise came out, a groaning, guttural sound. My face crumpled; my shoulders sagged. To my total mortification, my whole body was convulsed with terrible, shaking sobs.

For a moment that felt like an hour, Jessie stood there, gawping at me. Then she took my arm, none too gently, guided me to a bench and stuffed a pristine handkerchief into my hand. I wiped at my face, covering the cloth in a mess of tears, snot and grime, but no matter how hard I wiped, the tears didn't stop. And to be honest, it felt good to let them flow. It was as though a boil had burst and poisonous pus was pouring out of me, and all I felt was relief that I could finally let it go.

Jessie sat at the other side of the bench, well away from me. But she didn't storm off. She didn't sneer. She sat quietly, waiting, and when I finally stopped greeting, she spoke.

'I need to understand what you're so upset about, so tell me everything. Start at the beginning.'

I took a deep, gulping breath and I told her.

'My name's James Muir. I'm known as Jim.'

'I'm Jessie Wylie Rowat, but being a spy, I expect you know that already. Go on.'

'Stop interrupting me then. My father Frank was a weaver. His handloom took up one whole room in our cottage in Shuttle Street. He was good at his job. My ma always boasted that you couldn't tell his shawls from those made in Thibet and Kashmir. I worked for him as his draw boy, but I was a half timer at school. I can read.'

'I didn't doubt it. Frank Muir... I think I remember Papa mentioning that name. Did he do commissions for Rowat's?'

I clicked my tongue, exasperated by her constant interruptions.

'If you listen, I'll tell you. Your father visited us one day. Ma carried on so much, you'd have thought Prince Edward had dropped in for tea. Mr Rowat said he admired my father's shawls. He suggested that Dad should come an' work for him. My father talked it o'er wi' Ma. He'd no longer be his own boss, but he'd be getting a regular wage, instead of fightin' to be paid for commissions from merchants. It used to be a good life being a Paisley weaver, but it was gettin' harder and harder, an' he was workin' the same hours for a tenth of the pay by that time.'

I stopped to take a breath.

'That doesn't seem fair,' said Jessie. She twisted her bonnet strings, her eyes uneasy.

I pulled a face; amazed at her naivety.

'Where've you been living? Cloud-cuckoo land? When was life ever fair? Anyway, he would be usin' the factory looms, so could sell the cottage, rent a cheaper place. Ma agreed it would be for the best. An' I was a' for it, though nobody asked, because if Dad was usin' a Jacquard loom, he'd have no need for a draw boy, so I could look for paid work. I was keen to work as a groom or an ostler, anything wi' horses, but got a job as a piecer in the mill, in the meantime. So, Dad started work at the factory an' after a time he sold the cottage an' we moved into the flat in St James Street.'

Jessie's eyes brightened.

'My goodness, we were neighbours! We lived there too, until last month, when we moved in with Grandma Rowat.'

'Aye, well, I expect your house was fancier than ours.'

She must have noticed my eye-roll, because her smile slipped and the anxious, wary look returned to her eyes.

'For a while, all was well. My father enjoyed the company of working with other weavers and with the lassies in the finishing rooms. He was impressed with the Jacquard looms, liked the way he could change the patterns by simply changing a punched card. But all his skill counted for nothing when the company's customers stopped buying Paisley shawls. Your father closed R. T & J Rowat's when it stopped making him money. And my father was out of a job.'

Jessie looked away from me, pulled at a loose thread on her skirt.

'To be fair, Jim, what else could my father do?' she sighed, her voice so low she was hard to hear. 'He was facing ruin. It was hard for him too.'

I was about to snap that my heart bled for him, but I saw the conflicted, unhappy look on her face. She was trying to understand, but how could she?

'Ma says the bosses never lose. She says your father has fingers in plenty of other pies. But after Dad lost his job at the factory our lives slowly fell apart at the seams, like a badly stitched jacket.'

'But there are thread mills all over Paisley. Couldn't your father get work at the Clark or Coats Mills?'

Jessie turned towards me and her eyes were pleading, desperate for me to agree, but I couldn't tell her lies just to bring that joyous smile back, however much I was tempted. I shook my head.

'The thread mills employ mainly lassies an' the pay's terrible."

I decided to be completely honest.

'An' my father's pride got in the way: when he couldn't get another job as a weaver, he sank into an awfy gloom. Some days he wouldn't get out of bed, an' if he did, it was to go to the public house. I was too young to get a job that would pay more than pennies. Dad kept sayin' we needed to emigrate, but Ma felt that wee Agnes would never survive a long sea crossing to Canada or New Zealand. We struggled on, but when we lost our home, because we couldn't pay the rent, we were right out o' options. So, it was the poorhouse or starve...'

My voice faded away, as if it couldn't bear the shame.

'What happened next?' whispered Jessie. 'What happened to your family?'

I took another huge breath and I told her that too.

'I'm so sorry,' she said, as I finished. Tears were spilling down her cheeks. 'That's dreadful. No wonder you're angry with us.'

'I'm no' angry wi' you. You've got me a' wrong. I just need to get our money back.'

Jessie's hands fluttered in her lap. She twisted the fabric of her dress.

'I'll speak to my father,' she said. 'I'm sure he'll be

only too willing to help your family. He's on the boards of several charitable organisations.'

I opened my mouth to growl at her, but breathed deeply, kept my voice even.

'I don't want charity. I only want what's ours.'

Jessie looked away again. She wrung her hands. I could tell she didn't know whether to believe me.

Behind us, a loud female voice boomed. We both jumped. Jessie shifted to the furthermost edge of the bench.

'Surely that isn't that same girl? Do you see her, Edith? Over there on the bench, beside a street urchin!'

Two old ladies were standing at the park entrance. One of them pointed her parasol in our direction and Jessie groaned.

'Oh no. It's those nosy old bats again.'

She stood up, looked me straight in the eyes.

'I need to go, Jim. Come to Rosehill's back gate tomorrow evening about 5 o'clock. The gardener will have gone home by then and Bobby has riding lessons on Tuesdays. We'll get this sorted out. Rowats don't break their promises.'

Then she ran for it, bolting down the street, clutching her bonnet, her dark hair streaming behind her. The two old ladies walked past my bench, ignoring my presence, cawing to each other like a pair of crows.

I was left alone again, but now I was holding tight to a thread of hope.

Chapter 15

Jessie

The sun was sinking behind the trees as I hurried up the hill towards Rosehill. With every step, the weight inside me seemed to get heavier. If the boy was right, and surely he couldn't have faked such distress, then when my father had closed the shawl factory he'd wrecked the Muir family's lives. And what if they hadn't been the only ones? It didn't seem possible. My father was well known as a kindly soul, the definition of a gentleman. He wouldn't have deliberately hurt anybody, I was sure of it. But he had closed the factory. He had put all those people out of a job. And the boy was right; my family hadn't suffered for it. Some of our employees had clearly suffered terribly. Shame burned my cheeks as I realised that I had never given those poor people a thought.

Esther stood at the front door, eyes narrowed. arms folded across her scrawny chest.

'You're late! Where have you been? I've been worried

sick. I was about to go in and tell your father you were missing.'

'Well, there's no need now, is there? I'm back.'

I dodged past her, into the high-ceilinged hall, with its chandelier and chequered black and white tiles.

'Don't you take that tone with me, missy!'

Esther chased after me, her clumpy boots clashing on the tiles. She caught me at the parlour door and blocked my way.

'Get up those stairs! There's a bath run, but if you're late, you're last, so the water's not as warm as it was and not as clean either. You'd think young Robert had spent his day down a pit hauling coal.'

'I am not getting into Bobby's bathwater,' I said, shuddering at the thought. 'And anyway, I need to speak to Papa.'

Before Esther could stop me, I threw open the parlour door and marched in. Miss Arbuckle and Papa were sitting on either side of a flickering fire. My grandmother snored, mouth wide open, in her rocking chair. Miss Arbuckle perched on her seat, nursing a tot of whisky. Papa was engrossed in his Glasgow Herald. They looked up, faces registering astonishment, when I entered. I wasn't supposed to be there, I knew that. I was meant to be in the nursery with the other children, in Esther's charge. This was adult time, and it was meant to be sacrosanct, except in the direst of emergencies.

Papa recovered his voice first.

'My dear, it's after nine,' he said, glancing at the clock on the mantelpiece. 'Are you feeling poorly? Is Esther not around?'

Behind me, Esther gasped. She barged past me into the parlour.

'I'm right here, sir!' she said, stating the obvious in her determination not to be blamed for this calamity. 'I don't know what's come over her. I've told her it is past her bedtime, but she's insisting that she needs to speak to you!'

Esther tugged at my arm, trying to pull me backwards out of the room.

'It's urgent, Papa!'

'What on earth's going on? Is the child delirious?' barked Miss Arbuckle, downing her whisky in one gulp. 'Perhaps you need to lock the nursery door, William. It never did me or my sister any harm. And while I am on the subject of your undisciplined offspring, your son has been trampling on the begonias again. He needs a firmer hand, I tell you!'

Papa sighed. He put down his newspaper and got to his feet.

'I'm sure being beaten soundly with a belt never did you any harm either. *No immediately obvious harm at any rate.* Come, Jessie. We'll have this "*urgent*" discussion in the library, shall we?'

The library didn't really deserve its title. It was a tiny room furnished by two tall bookcases and a couple of battered leather chairs. My father sat down in one and beckoned for me to sit in the other.

I took a deep breath and let the words spill out as I exhaled.

'Papa, when you closed the shawl factory, people lost their jobs didn't they? Did you do anything to help all the people who used to work there? Did you do anything at all?'

My father's eyes wrinkled with anxiety.

'What's brought this on, Jessie? Did someone accost you while you were out on your walk? It was foolish of me to allow you to go unaccompanied.'

I shook my head, suddenly afraid that if I mentioned Jim I would make more trouble for him, when he seemed to have more than enough problems already.

'No, nobody accosted me. But I passed a homeless boy begging on the street and I suddenly worried that perhaps when Rowat's closed and people didn't have work, they might not have been able to pay their rent, that perhaps people lost their homes. I'd hate to think we caused anyone harm.'

My father patted my hand, but he no longer looked me in the eye. His eyes were fixed on the Persian rug at our feet.

'My dear, I am so proud that you have a kind heart,

and good socialist impulses, but you mustn't worry about such things at your tender age. It was a terrible time for all concerned, but we got through it. Most of the people we employed got jobs in the thread mills and bleaching fields. No one came to any lasting harm, I assure you. Now, is there anything else, or can I return to my newspaper?'

I shook my head. I was desperate to ask about the Muir family and about Frank Muir's missing money, but how could I, without telling Papa about Jim?

He ushered me out, and I headed upstairs. But his earlier words to Miss Arbuckle echoed in my brain.

No immediately obvious harm at any rate.

Maybe my father hadn't known that anyone had been hurt by the factory's closure. Or maybe he'd shut his eyes to the grim reality.

The following day at school I was tired and distracted; eager to get home. Bobby was in a hurry too. He loved his riding lessons at Prospecthill, our uncle's villa, and it was an easy trip from the house at Rosehill. When we arrived home, Bobby raced to the kitchen and stuffed his pockets with apples for Phoebe, the fat little pony who had been ridden by Uncle Thomas's nine children and now had to suffer my brother.

Esther always accompanied Bobby to his lessons, even though Prospecthill was only next door. Uncle Thomas's gardener was much younger and more handsome than Old Tam. And wherever Esther went, Mary went too. She loved to feed the pony (and herself) on sugar lumps.

I was anxious to avoid being asked to read the newspaper aloud to Miss Arbuckle. I needed a good excuse to go outside, so when I saw the withered flowers on the dining room table, I snatched them from their vase.

'I'm going to pick flowers for the dining table,' I told Esther. She was busy bundling Mary into the big perambulator, and scolding Bobby for having a dirty face.

'That's a good idea, Jess. I noticed the ones in the vase were past their best, but I've been rushed off my feet today.'

She spat on to her handkerchief and wiped it across Bobby's cheek.

'There, that's better. Hold on a minute, Jessie.'

She rummaged in a drawer and pulled out the secateurs. 'Take these, and if you're picking roses watch out for thorns. My sister Nellie died of a scratch that turned septic.'

Esther smiled at me as she handed me the secateurs, and I knew I was forgiven, which made me feel even more guilty about what I was about to do.

I waved them off, ensured Miss Arbuckle was safely in the parlour and headed into the kitchen.

Cook was red-faced, sweat trickling down her plump cheeks.

'When are you going to get that thing out of my way?' she asked, pointing at the easel in the middle of the room and a still life painting of cabbages and an earthenware jug that I was working on,

'I'm going to finish it tonight,' I told her, as I opened the back door.

'Well, you'll need to paint by memory because I need that cabbage for the main course and the jug for the custard.'

The back garden was long and walled, divided into sections by trellises and meandering gravel paths. The flower borders bloomed with late June flowers: lupins, foxgloves and delphiniums. Fat bumble bees droned, warmed by the sunshine and dragonflies skittered across the pond. It felt like a safe haven and I stopped on the path, reminded of the story of Pandora's Box. By opening the back gate, I was allowing trouble to come crashing in.

The shed door creaked as I opened it. Inside it smelled musty and was crammed with pots and garden tools. The key hung on a hook. I snatched it and dropped it in the pocket of my pinafore.

Clutching a bunch of blue delphiniums, the secateurs held like a weapon, I reached the gate. I glanced towards the house, but could only see the right hand corner. Nobody in the kitchen should have been able to spot me. Half hoping that the boy wouldn't be there, I put the flowers and the secateurs down, and took the key from my pocket.

Old Tam always padlocked the gate at night, saying the bolt wasn't sufficiently secure. With shaking fingers, I unlocked it, unwound the chain and drew the bolt. Unlike the shed door, the well-oiled gate opened smoothly. And I jumped like a startled frog, because the boy was standing on the path, right in front of me.

His expression was grim, his whole stance defiant. I got the impression that if I slammed the gate shut, he would stay exactly where he was until I opened it again.

But then he smiled at me and everything changed. His brown eyes sparkled and small dimples appeared in his cheeks.

'You took your time.' Jim brushed his hand over his unruly mass of hair, as if attempting to smooth it into tidiness. 'I thought you weren't comin'.'

'It's not easy to get away. I'm surrounded by family,' I said, and then felt a blush creep up from my neck, because that seemed a cruel thing to have said. To make amends, I reached into my pinafore pocket and handed him the bread roll I'd stolen from the kitchen table on my way out.

He took it, watching me all the time. Anxious that we

remain unseen, I sat down in the arbour by the back gate and beckoned to him to sit beside me. The air was warm, and bees buzzed in the sweetly scented honeysuckle entwining the arbour. I could almost imagine that nothing had changed in the garden, that I hadn't let a stranger enter, if it hadn't been for the sour odour emanating from the boy and for the revolting noises he made as he wolfed down the bread.

When he finished eating, I spoke, faking a confidence I didn't feel.

'Right, I don't have long. Tell me about the money. If my father owes your family back wages, then I suggest you write him a letter. He'll reimburse you immediately, I assure you.'

He shook his head so hard, his springy curls bounced across his forehead.

'I'm no' talkin' about lost wages. I'm talkin' about the coins which my dad sewed into a shawl. A shawl that was meant for my ma and which your father took as a gift for your ma instead...'

'I don't understand. Why did your father sew coins into a shawl?'

'My dad got some cash for the sale o' his handloom. The shawl was to be a surprise gift for my ma, to celebrate a new home an' a new job. Before we moved he spent every night for two weeks weavin' the shawl, the last on his own loom, for my ma. I helped him wi' it. Ma wasn't allowed into the loom room. The night afore the new tenant moved in and took o'er the loom, Dad sewed the coins in secret into the cloth's underside. It was to be Ma's emergency money, in case anythin' ever happened to him. Then he bundled the shawl in brown paper and took it wi' him when we moved into the St James Street flat.'

'The bank would have been safer,' I pointed out, but he ignored me.

'The shawl wasn't as perfect as Dad wanted, so he took it to the factory and asked the girls in the finishin' room to snip the loose threads. Your father was visitin' the works that mornin'. He saw the shawl, said it was the most beautiful he'd ever seen and took it as a gift for your ma's birthday. My dad couldn't complain, couldn't say a word, as he'd already started workin' for your father and he had used Rowat thread to make my ma's gift. I'm not sayin' that was right. I'm not askin' for the shawl back. But the money is ours. I need it, to save my family.'

There was such despair in his eyes that I spoke without thinking about the consequences.

'We'll get it back! You and me.'

I beamed at him, trying to get him to share my enthusiasm.

'I'll smuggle you into the house and we'll find your money. Then you can save your family from the poorhouse.'

He pulled a face.

'How's that goin' to work? Your house is full o' folk.'

I tugged at his sleeve, which was a mistake, because the fragile cotton tore.

'Follow me, but keep out of sight!'

Leaving the back gate swinging open, so he could make his escape when necessary, I headed back towards the house, carrying my delphiniums and the secateurs. When I got near the house, I beckoned to Jim to hide behind the honeysuckle arbour, and called out.

'Mrs Moore! Quick! Come quickly!'

Cook rushed outside, red-faced, her hair dusty with flour.

'Come and look!' I shouted, though I had no idea what I was going to show her.

She bustled over to where I stood, waving my hands like a windmill, by the garden pond.

'Get out of here as soon as her back is turned,' I hissed, hoping Jim could hear me. 'Go through the kitchen, take a left turn and head upstairs. I'll meet you in the nursery. That's the third door down the corridor on the left; it's the room with the rocking horse.'

Cook ran up and held on to a tree, gasping for breath.

'Who were you talking to, Jessie?' she said, staring round, eyes bewildered.

'I was calling on you! I just saw the biggest dragonfly ever! It was the size of a pterodactyl. Look over there in the centre of the pond. Can you see it too, Mrs Moore?'

She stared at me as though I'd lost my wits.

'I'm in the middle of cooking the dinner, you daft lassie! Are your father and grandmother to starve so that I can gawp at beasties in a pond? I thought you'd found a deid body floatin' in the wattir!'

I stood on tiptoe, balancing on a paving stone to seek out the non-existent dragonfly.

'I can't see it anymore. It must have flown away. It's a shame because I'd love to have sketched it. Their iridescent wings are glorious.'

I glared at Cook, pretending annoyance.

'Even my still lifes won't stay still. I bet you've shredded my cabbage.'

Cook made a noise like a trumpeting elephant.

'You'd better get those flowers in a vase. They're startin' to wilt,' she snapped and hurried back to the kitchen.

My insides churned.

I had no idea if Jim had made it into the house or not.

I followed Cook into the kitchen, stuffed the blooms into a tall vase and carried them into the dining room, past the closed parlour door. Hopefully, Miss Arbuckle and Grandma Rowat were enjoying their pre-dinner sherry too much to move from their chairs.

I scurried upstairs, glancing at the grandfather clock in the hall. It was nearly half past five. Papa wouldn't be home for another hour. I should be safe enough for a little while yet, I figured, unless Miss Arbuckle came snooping.

I tiptoed into Papa's room, lifted the shawl from the chair and carried it into the nursery. But there was nobody there. The room was empty.

Chapter 16

Jim

When I stepped out from behind the curtain, Jessie screamed, then clamped her hands across her mouth.

'You gave me such a fright,' she hissed. 'Stop sneaking up on me!'

'What was I meant to do? Sit on the edge o' the bed and hope your mother didn't come in to plump the pillows?'

Jessie turned away from me, and dropped the bundle she was carrying on to the floor by the window.

'You really don't know as much about my family as you think you do.' Her voice sounded muffled. 'My mother died two years ago.'

I didn't know what to say. I'd spent all week envying this girl's life, imagining she lived in a perfect, trouble-free bubble. But I had to think of something, for the silence was painful.

'I'm sorry. You and the weans must miss her a lot.'

'We all miss her. She was such fun, always laughing. Miss Arbuckle is the polar opposite of fun.'

'Is Miss Arbuckle the red-heided woman?'

Jessie shook her head.

'That's Esther. She's our housemaid and Mary's nanny. My mother's name was Margaret. This shawl belonged to—'

Jessie fell silent. She pulled the heavy drapes back as far as they'd go. Sunlight flickered through the glass and as she spread the shawl on the floor, its rich colours glowed with a soft sheen. I stared at it, and my mouth went bone dry, my palms clammy. For a second, I closed my eyes, remembering my father at his handloom in the cottage, the click of the shuttle as it whizzed to and fro across the warp threads, my mother's shawl taking shape as he worked. Dad and I made a lovely, soft as silk shawl for my mother; it was our final work on that loom.

But this shawl, the one Jessie was spreading on the floor, wasn't it.

It wasn't the shawl I'd helped my father make. I could remember *it* perfectly; a large field of forest green and a simple Paisley border in madder and indigo. This was a different shawl, with more colours and a far more intricate and sophisticated pattern, of flowers and swirls and twisted teardrops. I'd never seen this shawl before in my life. Something was terribly amiss. I rocked on my heels, swallowing hard. The desire to run was almost overwhelming. I'd been living on hope, and hope was shrivelling away.

I tried to remember exactly what my father said to me, as he lay dying on that metal cot in the Abbey Poorhouse.

"Rowat took the shawl I'd meant for your mother, as a present for his wife. It has our money in it, five guineas, the profit from the loom. You need to get it back, Jim. Promise me you'll get it back."

I shook my head, trying to clear the confusion. Nothing made sense. Was there another shawl I knew nothing about? Why would William Rowat take one shawl from my dad and give his wife another?

Jessie crouched down, and smoothed out the folds of the cloth. Her hands started to falter as she ran her fingers over the seams.

'There's nothing here, Jim,' she said, her voice so quiet I could hardly hear her. 'There are no hidden coins. I'd be able to feel their ridges, I'm sure I would. I'm so sorry.'

It was as if the shock stopped my heart. For a long moment I couldn't speak; couldn't breathe.

'They must be there! Dad said he'd sewn them along that bottom seam. There, on the right. Turn the cloth o'er. Perhaps you'll see them better on the underside.'

She shook her head, maddeningly certain.

'Are you sure you didn't misunderstand your father, Jim? Or if he was very ill, is it possible he was delirious?'

'I don't think so. I don't know. It has to be there.'

She looked up at me, and must have sensed my despair, because she went back to the shawl and kept trying.

Crouching down by her side, I worked my fingers into the cloth, down the seams and then, with increasing desperation, over the whole shawl and its underside. Finally, I admitted defeat. To be honest, I'd known as soon as I saw it. There were no coins sewn into that shawl; no hidden treasure. That shawl had nothing to do with me.

'You'd better put it back,' I said, trying to keep my voice from cracking.

Jessie didn't answer. She picked up a corner of the shawl. Her long, finely shaped fingers worked, tracing the threads on its underside. I started to back away, my mind focused on escape, on running as far from Rosehill as I could go.

'Look, Jim. I noticed this before, but it's clearer in the sunlight. These are letters. I'm sure they are. There's a message sewn into the cloth!'

Drawn back by a flicker of hope, I took the shawl's edge in one hand. In the right-hand corner, where I'd expected to find the hidden coins, tiny letters were stitched into the weave. They were almost impossible to see, but when I placed my fingertips over them I could trace each miniature letter shape. Letter by letter I spelled out the message aloud.

'Many Happy Returns.'

'I told you, Jim! This shawl was made for my mother's birthday.'

But I hardly listened to her. I spelled out the rest of the message and read it aloud,

'To Mrs Margaret Rowat, Made With Pride, James Muir.'

'It's a message from your father!' gasped Jessie. 'So, he knew when he made this shawl that it was meant for my mother! Why would he have sewn his own money into it, Jim? It doesn't make any sense!'

She's right, I thought. It doesn't make any sense at all.

But the message was a thin thread of comfort. This magnificent shawl was my father's handiwork and it was good to know he'd been capable of creating something so beautiful, something that would last longer than any of us.

Downstairs, the front door banged. I stared at Jessie, panic stricken, as I heard a dog's paws scrabbling across the tiled hall, boots clattering, and Esther calling Bobby.

'Come back and use the mud scraper! You're getting filth all over the rugs. Mary, my lamb, don't touch that glass case with those sticky fingers!'

'You need to hide,' hissed Jessie. 'Quick, get in here!'

She opened the wardrobe door; then shoved me toward it. I scrambled inside, pushing past the jackets, frocks and blouses on their padded hangers, kicking aside a leather satchel and a child's fishing net.

As Jessie closed the door, she gave me a shaky smile.

'You'll need to try and make a dash for it while we're at dinner. Listen for the gong.'

The door shut, and I was plunged into darkness. The wardrobe was stuffy, cluttered and reeked of mothballs, but it was warmer and cosier than most of the places I'd slept that week. I snatched a soft, furry garment from a hanger, placed it underneath my head, curled into a ball and tried to doze.

But my whirling thoughts wouldn't let me.

It was over. My dad must have been delirious, right enough. All my hopes had been shattered. My family's future was bleak. They only had two days left together. How would poor wee Andrew cope, all alone in the men's block? It was a horrifying thought. He was only a wean, far too young to be taken from his mother. It would kill Ma to lose him.

And what about me? What did my future hold, homeless and alone? Maybe I needed to leave Paisley, after all, and head westward, towards the coast.

I squeezed my eyes shut, focussing on memories, instead of a terrifying future. Dad always said he'd take me to the seaside one day. He said it wasn't far and we could get a train from Gilmour Street Station. Dad described the sea as a huge mass of foamy grey water, which didn't sound appealing, but I remember how Ma laughed and told Dad he was havering. She told us about the time she'd visited her Aunt Mina's in Saltcoats.

'It was a beautiful sunny day. We girls were so hot, that we begged to be allowed to take off our stockings and boots and go for a paddle. My mother wouldn't allow it, but my father overruled her. He rolled up his trousers and we all raced towards the sea, except my mother, who perched all afternoon, prim as you like on a deck chair, under her umbrella. At the shore, the water sparkled like pearls and was the colour of light mist. Far out, it was sapphire blue and as smooth as silk thread.'

Ma worked as a thread spinner at the Clark Mills as a lass and she never called colours by their ordinary names. Green was juniper or mint or emerald; blue was sapphire or cobalt or indigo. Her version was much prettier and I preferred it to Dad's. I could picture the scene as she described it: Ma and her sisters kicking the waves, soaking their best frocks with salty spray, squealing of joy, while my grandmother sat on her deckchair, stiff with disapproval.

Whatever the truth about the colour of the sea, I'd never been desperate to see it; I always stopped walking once I reached the outskirts of the town. Paisley was the only place I knew. I could hardly bear the thought of leaving my home town… I'd lost too many familiar things to be content to lose another.

But what else could I do? If I stayed in Paisley, scratching a living, I'd never manage to save enough money to rescue my family.

By the time I heard the gong's muffled clang, I'd come to a conclusion. My best option was to leave and start again somewhere else. Head for Greenock perhaps, and get work on a ship travelling to Europe or beyond. In another country, maybe I could start a new and better life. There was nothing left to keep me in Paisley. It was all over.

But I couldn't get away, couldn't even leave the bleedin' wardrobe, as I was no longer alone in the room. I could hear Jessie's voice, high and agitated, and an odd, rhythmic knocking sound.

'Esther, please stop banging that gong and come in here! I need a clean pinafore. Mine has a dirty mark. Is there one in the laundry room?'

'Calm yourself, lass. There's a freshly pressed one in the wardrobe.'

'No, wait! I'll get it.'

The door opened a sliver and a hand reached in, grabbing the pinafore from its hanger. The door banged shut and all I could hear was that rhythmic knocking sound.

'Bobby, get down from Wellington. We need to go!'

The gong clanged again. Boots stomped downstairs. The sudden quiet in the room was eerie.

I was clammy with sweat and the air was so stuffy, I felt as if I might suffocate. There was no handle on the inside, so I kicked open the wardrobe door, and gulped in fresh air.

At the top of the stairs, I stopped and waited, calculating my next move. The back door was impossible, as the kitchen was occupied. A window at the back of the house would be my best bet, then through the back garden and out the open gate.

But each time I went to move, the housemaid bustled out of the kitchen and into the dining room, on some errand or other. I started to feel panicky, knowing I was running out of time. It had to be now. Muscles tense, I watched Esther carrying a pitcher of water. As the door opened, I could hear an old lady's voice, high and quivery. A couple of minutes later, Esther shut the door behind her and hurried back to the kitchen.

Seizing my moment, I raced down the stairs, across the hall towards a door that I prayed wouldn't lead into a cupboard. The dog heard me and started barking. The kitchen door opened, just as I turned the handle and slipped inside.

To my huge relief, it wasn't a cupboard, nor a windowless box room. It was a room full of books. I ran a finger along the rows of spines: *Oliver Twist, Far from the Madding Crowd, Jane Eyre.*

Pulling myself away from a life which wasn't mine, I

opened the tall window and climbed out. Dropping on to the gravel, heart pounding, I started running and was almost at the back gate when the world started spinning and white stars flashed in my eyes. Dizziness overcame me and my legs crumpled. As I fell forwards, the sunlight faded to black.

Chapter 17

Jessie

During dinner, I couldn't eat Cook's cabbage and chicken creation, and not only because it was disgusting, the chicken stringy and the cabbage boiled to a muddy brown. I felt sick with nerves. Every creak made me jump, imagining that Jim was creeping down the stairs or through the hall, about to be caught by Esther, or overheard by Mack.

'Jessie, dear, I have asked you several times to pass the salt. Do you think you could do me the honour?'

'Sorry, Papa. Here you are.'

As our fingers touched, I looked into his kind eyes, and saw the way the skin round them crinkled when he smiled. I felt tears bubbling up. I wished I knew what had happened to the Muir family's money. I wished I could have helped them. And I wished that my lovely father hadn't been the one responsible for bringing disaster down on their heads.

'It's a beautiful evening,' announced Grandma Rowat, out of the blue. 'I think I might ride Laird across to Elderslie. William, will you ask Lewis to fit the side saddle?'

'Don't be so ridiculous!' snapped Miss Arbuckle. 'Lewis is long dead, and Laird's been dead even longer. You haven't ridden a horse for forty years. And it's not a beautiful evening. This warm weather will be the death of us both.'

She fanned herself with her napkin and scowled, sour as a lemon.

Grandma's hands fluttered round her face.

'Laird's dead? When did that happen?'

Wound up with nerves, my temper snapped. I glared at Miss Arbuckle.

'The other day you said the rain would be the death of you. Is there any weather which isn't potentially fatal?'

My father's eyebrows shot up.

'Jessie, I will not have you being rude to your elders!'

'Miss Arbuckle told Grandma not to be ridiculous. That was *really* rude,' piped up Bobby. 'When it's my birthday, may I have a horse? I could keep it in the shed.'

'I'll lend you Laird,' said Grandma Rowat, her eyes going misty. 'Fifteen hands of pure muscle. Brave as a lion.'

Bobby cocked his head to the side, thoroughly bemused.

'But Miss Arbuckle said...'

'Laird sounds incredible, Grandma Rowat,' I broke in hurriedly. 'You're so lucky to have your own horse.'

Miss Arbuckle opened her mouth, and I pushed my chair back, guessing she was about to send me to my room, and half hoping she would, because I was desperate to check if Jim had managed to get away safely.

But then Mack bolted from under the table. He threw himself against the dining room door, barking dementedly.

'Be quiet, you stupid animal!' bawled Miss Arbuckle, but Mack kept barking, beside himself with doggy rage. At that moment, Esther and Cook came in to clear the plates and serve up burnt rice pudding. As the door swung open Mack was catapulted backwards. He scrambled to his feet and shot out of the open door, yapping and snarling, charging towards his unseen enemy.

'What's up with Mack?' asked Papa, as we heard the dog's claws skittering along the hallway. 'Do you think there's someone at the back door?'

Bobby stopped flicking peas across the table.

'I expect it's the burglar, trying to get into the house.'

No, actually, I thought, *the burglar's trying to get out.*

'I'll go and see what's wrong,' I said. 'He probably heard a squirrel, or something.'

I found Mack in the hall, sniffing like a bloodhound round the bottom of the library door. When I pulled the door open, I saw why. The sash window had been pulled open. The curtains fluttered in the evening breeze.

Jim had gone, vanished back onto the streets; his dream of saving his family crushed. I'd promised to help him—and I'd failed.

Shushing Mack, I closed the window.

'Are you alright, Jessie?' asked Papa. 'You seem a little, um... unsettled... this evening.'

We were sitting in the parlour. It was the hour designated by Miss Arbuckle for *"family time"*. She watched the clock on the mantel religiously to ensure we didn't receive a second more attention than we were due. Mack, exhausted from his exertions, lay sprawled on a velvet cushion. Esther was building a tower of alphabet cubes, so that Mary could push them down. Every time the blocks toppled to the floor, Miss Arbuckle would wince and glance at the clock. Papa was showing Bobby how to play chess and I sat on the window seat, flicking through a copy of *Young Folks* magazine, totally unable to concentrate. I couldn't get Jim Muir out of my head, couldn't work out what to do next. I needed more information, and my father was the only one who could help.

'I'm fine, Papa. I was just thinking about Mama's shawl. The one you got her for her birthday. It's so beautiful. You must have been so pleased when you saw it being made.'

Bobby went still, his fingers hovering over the chessmen.

'Can I see it, Papa? Can I see the shawl you got for Mama?'

My father looked at Bobby, and his eyes softened.

'Yes, of course, you can, son. Your mother adored that shawl. I think she loved it more than the sapphire necklace I bought for her in Paris!'

He turned towards me, smiling at the memory, his eyes misty.

'You're right, Jessie. I *was* delighted when I saw the shawl being made. I went in several times to check on its progress. Frank Muir, our most skilled weaver, was in charge. He did a wonderful job. When I thanked him, he glowed with pride.'

He bent his head, ready to resume the chess game.

'Now, come on, young Robert. I hope you've got your strategies all planned out!'

I bit my lip. I couldn't stop now, even if Papa thought I was acting oddly. Even to my ears, my voice sounded peculiar, unnaturally bright.

'You told me that mother's shawl was the only one to be made from Kashmir goat hair in the factory. Wasn't there enough yarn to make any more?'

Papa looked up, his hand on a white knight. He didn't ask me to stop asking daft questions, but smiled at me, kind and patient as always.

'There was a little left over. I remember now.'

He put down the chess piece and turned towards me. Bobby pulled a face, annoyed that I was interrupting their game and taking Papa's attention away from him.

'When I was touring the factory, I asked about one of the shawls in the finishing room, as it was clearly not one of ours. I discovered that Muir had made another shawl on his own handloom, much smaller and of a simpler design, also from our Kashmir goat hair.'

'What did it look like?' I asked, trying to make my questions sound casual, and not like an interrogation.

'It was beautiful too, mainly forest green, but with a border of pines. It was almost as lovely as the one he'd made in the factory. When I asked him about it, he was worried I'd be upset he hadn't made it on a Jacquard loom in the factory.'

I swallowed hard, afraid to ask the next question.

'Were you angry?'

'At first, I was upset, naturally enough. Taking yarn home, particularly our precious Kashmir, was strictly against the rules. Muir was full of apologies; he told me he'd wanted to create something unique, a one-off shawl in his own design as a present for the Rowat family. I thought it was a very kind gesture, had both of them wrapped and delivered to the house, and made sure Muir got a bonus in his pay packet. So, it all ended well.'

I stood up, and the magazine in my lap tipped onto the floor.

'What happened to the other shawl?' I asked, in a voice which sounded squeaky and anxious. 'Did you give it to Mama too? Did she like it as much as the other?'

'Oh, I didn't give them both to your mother. Your Grandma Rowat got the handloom one. Didn't you, Mother?'

We both turned to my grandmother. My heart thudded in my chest. But my grandmother hadn't heard a thing. She grinned at me, mischief in her eyes, and she beckoned me over to look at the object in her hands. It was a long piece of white silk. She held it up in one hand and tapped the side of her nose with the other.

'I'm making you a pretty sash. We'll embroider poppies all over it: a crimson field of them.' She jerked her head towards Miss Arbuckle, and whispered: 'She's a bossy mare, that one, but she's not the boss of me.'

I bit my lip, to stop tears from spilling.

'You're the best grandmother in the whole world.'

I smiled at her and patted her fragile, liver-spotted hand.

Miss Arbuckle frowned and clicked her tongue.

'For goodness' sake, woman! William's asking about your shawl, not a sash!' she barked.

Grandma Rowat stiffened.

'There's no need to shout at me. I am neither deaf

nor stupid.'

When Miss Arbuckle snorted, my hand itched to slap her. But at the same time, I was desperate for Grandma Rowat to answer her question.

But Grandma's gaze clouded, and her jaw slackened.

'I haven't got a shawl,' she quavered. 'Why would I need such a thing? I wear my riding habit every single day. It's a beautiful evening. I think I might go for a ride on Laird'

Miss Arbuckle raised her eyes to the ceiling and got to her feet.

'The shawl will be in her closet. I'll go and get it,' she sighed.

I couldn't sit still when she went upstairs to look for the shawl. I walked over to the window seat again and gazed out of the window at the beech tree. Jim wouldn't be there. He'd be long gone. When Miss Arbuckle brought down the shawl, I'd find an excuse to try it on and check the seams. But even if I found the money, how was I ever going to find its owner?

The seconds ticked by. Bobby came over and sat beside me on the window seat.

'Will we restart this game, young Robert?' asked Papa, waving a pawn.

Bobby shook his head.

'No thanks. I might just go to bed now,' he said. 'I'm quite tired.'

This was such a weird comment that I turned and stared. Bobby's face was flushed. He was fidgeting and kept stealing glances at the door. Miss Arbuckle's boots clicked as she descended the stairs. She stood in the doorway, glowering.

'It isn't in her closet, or in the pine chest. Where on earth can it be?'

Bobby clutched at my sleeve.

'Help me, Jessie,' he whispered. 'Miss Arbuckle's going to kill me.'

'What's happened, Bobby? What have you done?'

'I know where the shawl is,' he whispered, anguish in his eyes. 'I took it. It's outside. But—'

'Show me.'

I stood up and grabbed his hand.

'Bobby has left his gird outside in the garden,' I announced. 'We're going to fetch it in case it rains. It's getting quite rusty, you see.'

I almost knocked Miss Arbuckle off her feet as I rushed past, dragging Bobby. Once we were outside I stopped and shook my brother by the arm.

'Where did you put the shawl, Bobby? Where is it?'

My finger nails must have been pinching his skin, because tears gathered in his eyes, but I was too wound up to care.

He pointed behind the garden shed, and it dawned on me. We started running across the lawn towards the laurel bushes.

By the time I'd squeezed into Bobby's den, my pinafore was smeared with dirt, my stockings torn. I crouched in the cramped space beside Bobby and looked around. Evening sunlight slanted through the laurels' glossy leaves, dappling the dusty ground. I could see why he liked it in here.

'It's a good den,' I told him, and his face brightened.

He tugged at a piece of cloth, covering the gap between two of the bushes. It was a large square of green cloth with a Paisley border, and had been attached to the bushes with lengths of knotted twine.

'I can pretend it's a pirate ship,' he confided. 'And the shawl is a sail. Yesterday it was a Sioux teepee.'

I took a corner in my hand, squeezing moisture from the cloth. It was filthy and stank of damp. It was the shawl Frank Muir wove for his wife, and our Bobby had ruined it.

'Oh, Bobby, why?' I asked, though it was a silly question. I could see perfectly well why. His den wasn't enclosed enough and the shawl did the job beautifully, as well as doubling as a sail.

'It was just lying there at the bottom of Grandma's closet. She wasn't using it,' he said, chin jutting.

'You'll need to give it back right now. Everybody's looking for it. We'll say we found it lying in the bushes. We can blame Mack, say he must have dragged it out here.'

145

Bobby's shoulders sagged as the tension left them. His eyes danced. Chirping like a canary, he helped me to untie the shawl. I was scarcely listening, trying desperately to think of a plan. As soon as it came down I'd check the shawl for hidden coins, before Miss Arbuckle could snatch it away to get laundered or binned.

Then, to my horror, a blood-chilling scream ripped through the evening air. Bobby squeezed his eyes shut and clutched my hand.

'Who's screaming?' he whispered, voice tight with anxiety. 'Tell them to stop, Jessie.'

I had no idea who was screaming until I heard Esther's voice: shrill, panicked.

'Help me, somebody! He's dead! Help me!'

Bobby's grip was so tight, he crushed my hand.

'Is it Papa?' he breathed. 'Is Papa dead like Mama?'

Chapter 18

Jim

The world swam back into focus. Last thing I remembered was falling on grass, but now everything was different. I was lying on a mattress, covered by a blanket, which felt soft and ticklish against my chin. All around me, no matter which way I turned, stood shelves of leather bound books. For a second I wondered if I'd died and this was heaven. But when I twisted my head further, I saw the tall window, fringed by blue velvet drapes, and I knew where I was.

Rosehill.

A man was sitting in the leather chair; a man with a dark beard and familiar, pale blue eyes. I knew him too.

'You're the man at the station. You gave me your lunch.'

The words came out muffled, as though my mouth was full of sawdust.

'Could I have a drink of water?'

The man nodded slowly.

'Ah, I thought we'd met somewhere before. I'm William Rowat. My daughter has gone to get you water. We could see you were waking. She has been telling me all about your situation. I believe I was keeping something of yours. Jessie unpicked the shawl's seam and retrieved these.'

He reached in his pocket and held out his palm. I counted five silver guineas. He piled them on a pine box beside the mattress.

'You gave our housemaid quite a scare. She thought you were dead, but Cook felt a pulse so we brought you in here, and called the doctor. You've been out for the count for almost twenty-four hours. But according to the doc, you're far from dead. There's nothing wrong with you that food and rest won't cure.'

A head peeped round the door, then another. Jessie and Bobby squeezed into the narrow room and stood round the mattress, gawping at me as if I was a monkey in a cage.

'Oh good, you're awake,' said Bobby. 'Did Papa give you the treasure? I found it. Well, Jessie found the coins, but I was the one who found the shawl. What are you going to do with it? I'd buy a horse, if I were you.'

'Bobby, leave him alone,' hissed Jessie. 'I've brought the water pitcher, Papa.'

I gulped down a glass of water, and another. Then

Esther appeared with a bowl of chicken broth. But although the Rowat family were being kindness itself, I didn't feel comfortable in their presence. These people came from a different world and although from a safe distance I'd imagined being part of it, now that I was in such close proximity, it felt too big a distance to bridge. And I needed to leave Rosehill because I had a job to do, and it was urgent. While I mopped up the remains of the broth with a hunk of bread, I tried to explain to them, without seeming rude.

'The money's to get my family out of the poorhouse,' I said. 'I need to go and get them. I need to get them now.'

Mr Rowat laid a hand on my shoulder.

'It's all in hand, lad. I've been in touch with the appropriate authorities this afternoon and your family's discharge papers have been signed. I've got business to attend to this evening but my cousin, Miss Arbuckle, has kindly agreed to collect your family and take them to a property I own in Lawn Street, where you may stay for as long as you need. You can accompany her tonight if you feel up to it. Otherwise, you are welcome to remain here.'

'We don't need charity.' I muttered. 'I've got money.'

'Believe me, this isn't charity. The guilt of closing the shawl factory and putting my employees out of work is keeping me awake at night. Allow me this, Jim.'

His eyes misted with tears. Jessie was right, her father did have a kind heart, but it was hard to feel pity for tears which could be wiped away with a monogrammed silk handkerchief. I was about to refuse, but thought of Andrew, being dragged away by the matron, and I swallowed my pride.

'If you can get us a place to live, then I'll be grateful. But we'll pay a fair rent.'

I struggled to my feet, and my face burned when realised I was half naked, dressed in a long cotton nightshirt.

'You'll look very silly going out like that,' Bobby sniggered.

Jessie prodded her brother with her elbow.

'It's alright Jim, don't pay him any attention.'

She held out a bundle of clothes.

'These were our cousin's. There should be something to fit you.'

'We'll leave you to get dressed,' said Mr Rowat.

As they were leaving, I clutched at Bobby's jacket sleeve.

'Could you do somethin' for me before I go, please? I've left some property in the tree in your front garden. Could you get it for me?'

In the early evening, Miss Arbuckle and I travelled down the hill towards the poorhouse in a carriage pulled by two silk-black geldings. Miss Arbuckle swept into the front office and I waited at the door. Within a couple of minutes, I heard her booming voice.

'I shall be speaking to the Parish Board! This place is filthy. Call yourself a matron? You are a disgrace, madam!'

Miss Arbuckle stormed out, my mother and siblings half running behind her. We all piled into the carriage. Ma sat, face stunned, twisting the fabric of her shift in her hands.

'What's happening, Jim?' she whispered. 'Where are we going? Where'd you get those clothes?'

'There's nothing to be alarmed about, Mrs Muir,' snapped Miss Arbuckle. 'Sit still, boy. If you fall headfirst from the carriage, there will be an almighty mess on the pavement.'

Andrew sat, statue still, hands clasped on his knees, gazing at Miss Arbuckle with awe-filled eyes for the remainder of the journey.

The flat in Lawn Street wasn't Rosehill; it was no palace, just a first-floor single end with a narrow window overlooking the back court. But it was spotless; whitewashed, with a gleaming range and a pristine mattress in the bed recess and on the truckle bed underneath.

Miss Arbuckle's eyes scanned the room. She clicked her tongue when she saw the bare mattresses.

'Put the trunk down here, Davis,' she said to the carriage driver, who had lugged a heavy pine trunk up a flight of stairs. 'I hope that foolish girl had the sense to pack bedding.'

She ran her eyes over Andrew and little Agnes, flicked her gaze upward and sighed deeply.

'And decent clothing.'

Then she went to the trunk and took out a parcel wrapped in brown paper. She turned to my mother, who was standing in the centre of the room, her expression caught between disbelief and elation, and she handed her the parcel.

'This is your rightful property, I believe. My cousin sends his sincere apologies for the misunderstanding. Good day. Come along, Davis. Stop dawdling.'

She swept out, her wide skirt brushing the floorboards.

My mother flopped down on the bed. I came and sat beside her, a bubble of happiness building in my chest.

'I tellt you, Ma, that I'd get you out of there. And I tellt you our new home wouldn't have bugs.'

Andrew came to life, scurrying round, checking the skirting boards for any signs of insect life. Agnes followed him, toddling on bare feet. I glanced towards the trunk, wondered if there were any cast-off shoes or boots in there that would fit her: but first things first.

'Open the package, Ma,' I said, poking at it with my finger. I guessed what it contained, but I hadn't seen this shawl since Dad and I had taken it from the loom.

The cloth spilled out across Ma's lap as she unwrapped

it. She fingered the soft Kashmir, stained only in a couple of places, after the scrubbing Esther gave it. The shawl was almost as good as new. I turned over a corner and read aloud the message Jessie had discovered when she was mending the fringe this afternoon.

To my wife Janet,
Made with love and pride,
Frank Muir

It was the first time I ever saw my mother cry.

Chapter 19

Jessie

Paisley is hardly a sprawling metropolis, but it is more than five years before Jim and I cross paths again. I'm cycling through Brodie Park on my new safety bicycle. It's a sunny August afternoon. My outfit, a scarlet jacket and matching bloomers, is causing quite a stir: an irritating mixture of sniggers and scandalised tuts. Two elderly ladies point at me, mouths pursed, and the memory of the two old dears accosting me in the Fountain Gardens comes flooding back. I'm so distracted that I fail to see the old man and his yappy terrier until I'm almost upon them. I swerve, my front wheel wobbles and I veer into the flowerbeds, tip over the handlebars and land heavily among the geraniums.

A young lad, roughly dressed, rushes over to help me up, though he's laughing so hard he's of scant use. I scramble to my feet, brush myself down and try and restore a semblance of dignity, while he examines my bicycle and declares it undamaged.

'Thank you so much,' I say, extending my hand. 'You are a true gentleman.'

'You're welcome, Jessie Rowat,' he replies.

Flustered, I stare rather longer than is generally considered good manners. His voice has deepened, his black curls are cropped short. But I look into his dark brown eyes and I remember.

'Jim Muir! Our burglar! What a delightful surprise,' I gabble. 'I hope your mother and sister and brother are well. You must come and visit. My father would be so pleased to see you!'

Jim smiles and agrees that he might, but we both know he won't. Jim Muir and I inhabit different worlds.

But as we walk together towards the park exit, wheeling my bike, I ask a question, while I've got the chance.

'Jim, what was it you were carrying about in that sack? The one you got Bobby to fetch for you from the tree? He has been puzzling over it all those years. Lucky you had tied it tightly, or he would have sneaked a peek.'

He shrugs and grins at me.

'Nothing of value: belongings o' my dad's. Things I thought would help me to remember him, like his shuttle, pipe, neckerchief and pattern book. It took me a long while to realise that I didn't need them, that he's right here.'

He taps his fingers to his chest and it dawns on me that I'm wrong, after all.

Jim's world and mine are just the same.

Author's Note

William Rowat built St Margaret's, his beautiful house in Brodie Park, and the family moved in when Jessie was 17. The following year, her uncle Robert Wylie Hill, took her to Italy, as promised. This visit inspired Jessie's interest in textiles and two years later she enrolled at the Glasgow School of Art, as did her sister Mary a few years after.

Five years later Jessie married the School's Head, artist Francis Henry aka Fra Newbery, and in 1894 she established an embroidery department at Glasgow Art School, an act which was hugely influential in raising the status of embroidery as an art form. Jessie was an inspirational teacher. She said 'I see education consisting of seeing the best that has been done. Then, having this high standard set before us, in doing what we like to do.'

Jessie also taught dress design and she designed and made beautiful but practical clothing for herself and her two daughters. She was one of a group of women artists known as the Glasgow Girls, a group which included Margaret and Frances MacDonald and Jessie King.

Jessie and Fra Newbery were close friends of Charles Rennie MacKintosh and his wife Margaret McDonal. Fra commissioned MacKintosh to build a new purpose-built premises for the Glasgow School of Art. The extended Rowat family commissioned other designs from MacKintosh, including a drawing room interior for their townhouse in Kingsborough Gardens and a fireplace for Prospect Hill House. In 1908 Jessie retired from work due to ill health and went to live in Dorset, where she continued to embroider until she died in 1948.

James Muir is an entirely fictional character, so what happened to him next is anyone's guess. I like to imagine that he emigrated to America, struck gold in California, bought a ranch and rode off into the sunset on a Palamino mare called Paisley, named after the town he loved.

Jessie Rowat Newbury

1864-1948

Reproduced courtesy of Glasgow Museums and the
artist's heirs

A Pattern of Secrets: The Tour

Stroll through the Fountain Gardens and admire Grand Central Fountain, which was restored in 2014 and features four life-size walruses!

GRAND CENTRAL FOUNTAIN.

Walk from Oakwood (former location of Paisley Grammar School), down School Wynd, along New Street and into County Place (now renamed County Square). The County Buildings and Prison on the right of the square have been replaced by a shopping centre, the Piazza. The hansom cabs have gone too but Gilmour Street Station is still there.

As you head towards Paisley Abbey, look for statues of George Clark and Peter and Thomas Coats, owners of Paisley's biggest thread mills. The Abbey welcomes visitors and has a cafe and gift shop.

Many of the street names in Paisley are reminders of the town's textile heritage. Look out for *Silk Street, Gauze Street, Lawn Street, Cotton Street, Thread Street, Miller Street, Shuttle Street* and *Dyers Wynd*.

If you have time, check out the exterior of St Margaret's in Brodie Park (William Rowat's family home has been recently converted into luxury flats).

Places to visit to find out more about Paisley's history in the textile industry:

Paisley Thread Mill Museum, Seedhill Road Paisley
Sma' Shot Cottages, Shuttle Street Paisley
The Weaver's Cottage, Church Street, Kilbarchan

Paisley Museum and Art Gallery in the High Street, has a fabulous Paisley Shawl collection and a recently constructed *Loom Gallery*. It also holds these paintings by Jessie's husband, Fra Newbery:

William Rowat
Miss Arbuckle
The Paisley Shawl

Photo p160: *Grand Central Fountain* by Maclue and Macdonald, Lithographera, Glasgow (Public Domain)

Photo p161: *Paisley Abbey* by © User:Colin / Wikimedia Commons, CC BY-SA 3.0, https://commons.wikimedia.org/w/index.php?curid=28719654

About the Author

Lindsay Littleson has four grown-up (ish) children and lives near Glasgow. A full-time primary teacher, she began writing for children in 2014 and won the Kelpies Prize for her first children's novel The Mixed Up Summer of Lily McLean. The sequel, The Awkward Autumn of Lily McLean, is also published by Floris Books.

In 2015 her WW1 novel Shell Hole was shortlisted for the Dundee Great War Children's Book Prize and she enjoyed engaging in research so much that she was inspired to write another historical novel, A Pattern of Secrets, this time focusing on her local area.

www.lindsaylittleson.co.uk

Acknowledgements

With grateful thanks to:

Anne Glennie at Cranachan Publishing, not only for her support and editing skills, but for designing such a stunning cover for A Pattern of Secrets.

The rest of the Cranachan authors, who are all so lovely I was desperate to join #ClanCranachan.

Denise Findlay and her family, for their enthusiastic response to the news that I'd written a children's novel about Jessie Rowat, Denise's great-great grandmother, and for giving permission for the use of Jessie's photograph.

The very helpful staff at Paisley Heritage Centre, Library and Museum. This book could not have been written without their help, inspiring exhibits and my fabulous map of Old Paisley, purchased at a bargain price from the museum shop.

Fiona Pollok and Robbie Donaldson for agreeing to read the novel and for being so kind and enthusiastic about it.

Julie Paterson, Literacy Development Officer at Renfrewshire Council, for emailing local schools and helping me to arrange author visits. As a full time teacher, I am incredibly grateful that my employers have been so supportive of my writing.

My partner, Ian, and my children, Sally, David, Matt and Emily. Thank you for putting up with me. You're all amazing. xx